"Other
like This
Alex?"
... *eel*
... *oes*

Brook gave him a bewildered look, still half-dazed by his kisses. Couldn't he tell he was the only man who had such a devastating effect on her? She looked into the hard face and knew she had little defense against him. She had to guard her heart now as she'd never guarded it before. Immediately she moved away.

His blue eyes surveyed her. "I don't like cat-and-mouse games," he drawled. "Let's be frank—what do you want in exchange for your favors?"

JEANNE STEPHENS
has been greatly encouraged with her writing career by her husband, who thinks she can do anything. She is a voracious reader and often takes long walks during which she works out her plot problems.

Dear Reader:

I'd like to take this opportunity to thank you for all your support and encouragement of Silhouette Romances.

Many of you write in regularly, telling us what you like best about Silhouette, which authors are your favorites. This is a tremendous help to us as we strive to publish the best contemporary romances possible.

All the romances from Silhouette Books are for you, so enjoy this book and the many stories to come. I hope you'll continue to share your thoughts with us, and invite you to write to us at the address below:

Karen Solem
Editor-in-Chief
Silhouette Books
P.O. Box 769
New York, N.Y. 10019

JEANNE STEPHENS
Sweet Jasmine

Silhouette *Romance*
Published by Silhouette Books New York
America's Publisher of Contemporary Romance

Other Silhouette Books by Jeanne Stephens

Mexican Nights
Wonder and Wild Desire
Bride in Barbados
Pride's Possession

SILHOUETTE BOOKS, a Simon & Schuster Division of
GULF & WESTERN CORPORATION
1230 Avenue of the Americas, New York, N.Y. 10020

ISBN: 0-671-57189-3

First Silhouette Books printing November, 1982

10 9 8 7 6 5 4 3 2 1

Map by Ray Lundgren

For Jo, Clayton,
Beth and Julie

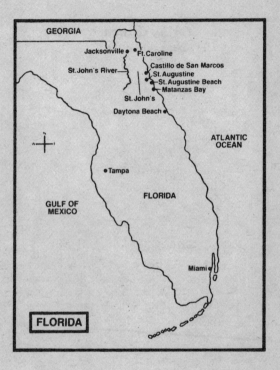

GEORGIA

Jacksonville • Ft. Caroline

St. John's River

Castillo de San Marcos
• St. Augustine
St. Augustine Beach
• Matanzas Bay

St. John's

Daytona Beach •

ATLANTIC
OCEAN

• Tampa

FLORIDA

GULF OF
MEXICO

Miami •

FLORIDA

Chapter One

Nowhere else was there an aroma so heavenly as the smell of St. Augustine in May. Brook stood on the second-floor balcony of her hotel room, her slender fingers curled around the wrought-iron railing, and gazed out across the beach over the still, gray-green waters of Mantanzas Bay to Anastasia Island, where the white walls of another hotel glistened in the first glorious rays of the sunrise.

The air was laden with the sweet scent of jasmine. The lush vines with their delicate white blossoms grew in abundant profusion all over town. Called Confederate Jasmine by southerners, the flowering shrub gave off an aroma that was, to Brook, lovelier than the most expensive French perfume.

It had been four years since her earlier visit to St. Augustine; she had come here on a two-week vacation with her parents after her graduation from the Kansas City Art Institute. Now, on this first morning of her second visit, the gracious atmosphere of the old town was casting its unique spell over her again in a way that no other town had ever done.

It was an enchanted place, Brook thought, as she looked forward to the coming weeks with a contented sigh. She had come to St. Augustine to do the illustrations for a children's book about the town's early history. The book had been written by a Newbery Award–winning author with whom Brook had worked on a previous book, and the publisher planned a heavy promotional campaign when the volume was released late next year.

Idly she brushed thick, tumbled black hair away from dark-lashed gray eyes and smiled to herself. After three years of working for an ad agency in Kansas City and scrambling for free-lance illustrating jobs on the side, she had ten months ago arrived at a point where she could quit the agency and go into illustrating full-time. Since her graduation from the institute, she had built a reputation for herself as an illustrator of children's books, and lately there had been so many offers she had actually been able to pick and choose the jobs that appealed to her most—like this one in St. Augustine.

Moreover this job couldn't have come at a better time, allowing her, as it did, to escape from Rob McAnnally, with whom she had worked at the ad agency and who, after dating Brook casually for two years, would not believe that she actually meant to refuse when he finally got around to proposing marriage. He seemed to think that she only wished to be persuaded and he had been making a nuisance of himself the past few weeks. He had even gone to talk to her parents in an effort to enlist their aid in getting Brook to set a wedding date.

Brook's mother had made a special trip across town to her daughter's apartment to talk about Rob, an action so uncharacteristic that it had jolted Brook into realizing that although her parents had allowed her to live her own life for years now, they hadn't stopped worrying about her.

Her mother's tone had been half-apologetic as, seated in Brook's living room, she had said, "Darling, Rob is such a nice young man—and you *are* twenty-five."

Brook had laughed at the anxious frown on her mother's face. "You sound as if I'm ready for Social Security!"

Her mother had quickly demurred. "That didn't come out quite as I'd intended." She gazed fondly at her daughter. "Oh, I know it's none of my business, but I can't help feeling concerned about you. Your father and I aren't getting any younger and you're our only child—and, well, we would like to see you settled, with a family." A wistful expression touched her eyes. "I've always dreamed of watching my grandchildren grow up."

"Mother!" Brook exclaimed. "You can't expect me to marry just to give you grandchildren! I don't love Rob."

Her mother's frown was back, deeper than before. "I don't understand you sometimes. The older you get, the more particular you are. Sometimes I think you're looking for something that doesn't exist—a romantic dream. Your father's sister was like that, and you see where it got her."

Brook smiled. "Spare me another rehash of the reasons for Aunt Sarah's spinsterhood. Besides, she's always seemed to me to be quite happy with her life. The last time I heard from her she was conducting a group of senior citizens on a tour of Greece and having a grand time."

Seeing that this line of reasoning was not furthering her cause, her mother tried another tack.

"Rob is a fine man. He'll make some lucky girl a good husband."

Brook tossed her black hair impatiently and sat forward on the edge of her chair. "I'm sure you're right, Mother—some *other* girl, not me." She spoke earnestly, wanting her mother to understand so that she would stop worrying. "He wanted me to quit work. Did you know that?"

Her mother looked nonplussed. "Why, I'm sure it's only because he's ready to start a family."

Brook made a sarcastic sound. *"He's* ready. Don't you think he should have consulted me about it? We've never even discussed it, you know. Anyway, there's a lot more to it than Rob's wanting a family."

"You ought to be grateful that he wants to take care of you. Lots of women would give their eye-teeth for a man like that."

Brook raised an eyebrow at her mother's innocence. "It has nothing to do with his wanting to take care of me, either, Mother. He can't accept the fact that I'm more successful in my career than he is. Even if I loved him, I could never marry a man who's so unsure of his own worth that he resents the satisfaction my work gives me. It's the most important thing in my life and—"

Her mother interrupted her with a clucking sound. "Precisely my point, dear. You need more in your life than work."

Following that talk with her mother, which Brook suspected had been duly reported to Rob, he had left her alone for a week, no doubt giving her time to come to her senses. Then he had arrived at her apartment to find her packing to leave town. He was incensed.

Trailing her into the bedroom he demanded, "How long have you known about this trip? Don't you think you owed me the courtesy of at least letting me know about it?" Brook's wordless shrug seemed to anger him further. "You were really going without saying anything to me, weren't you?"

Brook continued to fold clothes into a suitcase spread open on her bed. "I felt we had already said all there was to say to each other." Then in an attempt to soften the finality of the words, she added, "It's best this way, Rob. I'm sure you'll find someone else—someone more suited to you."

He glowered at her. "You bet your life, I will! Brook, you're going to wake up one day and discover you've grown old alone."

Brook sighed with exasperation. She had wanted to part from Rob on amicable terms. She'd even hoped they could continue to be friends. "Aren't you being a bit melodramatic?"

"On second thought," he sneered, "you might not even notice you're alone! I've always suspected you're cold and unfeeling. Now I'm convinced of it. You're not a woman, you're an illustrating machine!" With that, he had turned on his heels and slammed out of the apartment.

An illustrating machine! Brook could still hear the scorn in Rob's accusation and, even though she realized he had merely wanted to hurt her, it continued to sting.

Padding barefoot across the balcony, she reentered the large hotel room, thinking that, in one way, Rob might be right. Was she *too* independent? The few men she had dated since her art school days had been made clearly uncomfortable by Brook's single-minded dedication to her career. Rob, in fact, had been more tolerant than most of them. It was her sudden success this past year that he hadn't been able to handle.

She crossed to the closet and, tossing aside her robe and nightgown, put on a cotton jumpsuit and flat, backless straw sandals. Then, sitting at the dressing table as she brushed her thick hair away from a center part and applied a dash of lip gloss, she studied her fine-boned face with detached interest. The high cheekbones, straight nose, arching black brows, sooty lashes, and cool gray eyes combined to make what she had been told was "a model's face." At any rate, Brook's face and slender, full-breasted figure seemed to attract men. The problem was that most of them were soon put off by her natural reserve and serious outlook.

Brook had never troubled herself to be more outgoing, to play at being the party girl that most men of her acquaintance seemed to prefer. She despised people who pretended to be what they were not. So perhaps she *would* have to live her life alone. Certainly that would not be as unpleasant as being trapped in a marriage that stifled her.

Unexpectedly a sudden chill skipped up her backbone, causing her to shiver. She shrugged aside her depressing thoughts as she prepared to leave the hotel. She would go for a stroll on the beach before breakfast. She picked up her sketchpad and some drawing pencils, dropping them into a large straw shoulder bag as she went out the door.

Early as it was, several joggers were running along the sandy path across the avenue from her hotel. Brook strolled slowly up the beach, staying out of the path of the joggers, and shortly found herself near the Bridge of Lions, which connected the mainland with Anastasia Island. She walked onto the bridge and, standing on the cement walkway out of the path of cars, leaned against the railing and looked down at the cabin cruisers and fishing boats that were lined up along the dock.

There was even one yacht, looking rather like a swan among a flock of mudhens. The white craft was long and sleek, with the name "Aphrodite" painted on its stern. Some rich man's toy, she thought, it had probably cost more than most people's houses. But maybe the yacht was his home—ready to move on to the next exotic place whenever the present one began to pall, for any man who could afford such a vessel probably didn't have to stay in one place and work for a living. In her mind she pictured the yacht's owner—sun-darkened, probably overweight from too much rich food, and at the core shallow, selfish, and overly impressed with himself.

Then she smiled at her flight of fancy. She couldn't let her experiences with the men in her past lead her to put all men in an uncomplimentary light. Surely they weren't *all* like Rob. Losing interest in the yacht, she let her glance drift to the far shore of the bay.

On a narrow strip of sand skirting the island, a flock of pelicans had gathered. As she watched, three of the birds flapped their wings and rose to skim across the bay below the bridge; their bodies, large and awkward in repose, were transformed in flight to a fluid gracefulness. Abruptly her artist's imagination saw a picture—a few pelicans at rest, others airborne. It had the sort of contrast she liked. She wanted to sketch the birds and continued walking at a fast clip across the bridge on the walkway to the island side.

Leaving the bridge, she picked her way through tall weeds near the shoreline, moving slowly so as not to startle the pelicans who gabbled to each other on the sandbar just off shore.

It took several minutes to find a dry, level spot of sand where she could sit. She settled herself quietly, keeping an eye on the pelicans a hundred yards away, and took out her sketchpad and a drawing pencil. She was soon lost in studying the birds and making quick sketches one after the other, unaware of the humid atmosphere and increasing warmth as the sun rose higher.

It was perhaps a half hour later when she heard someone approaching, tromping loudly through the weeds and making no effort at all not to disturb the pelicans. She turned and saw a man coming toward her.

Before he said a word, she knew exactly what she could expect from him. His blue-black eyes flicked over her in an insolent summing up, the hard mouth grimly cynical, sun-bleached blond hair falling across his forehead and raking his collar with a blatant disregard for neatness, the long, sun-bronzed body moving with effortless power like a well-oiled machine.

When he reached her and stood, his long legs in tight, faded jeans planted firmly apart, his first words only confirmed her previous impression.

"What are you doing?"

There was a commotion of squawking and flapping on the sandbar as the pelicans took flight, frightened by the loud voice.

It did seem as though it were her destiny to meet all the unpleasant males in the world, for this stranger was everything she resented in a man—rude and bullying, with an air of male superiority so palpable she could have cut it with a knife.

She looked up at him with steady gray eyes. "I should think that would be obvious," she retorted with as much ice in her tone as she could possibly inject.

She saw a flicker of surprise in the disconcerting, midnight-blue eyes. Then thick, honey-colored lashes came down as the eyes narrowed. "You're trespassing on private property." His tone indicated he was accustomed to ordering people about.

She glanced over his shoulder and, for the first time, noticed the sprawling outlines of a partially constructed building, probably a hotel. There was no sign of any other workmen as yet, and she decided he must be a foreman. He was the sort of man who would be on the job before anyone else and stay after the others had gone home. She understood that sort of dedication, but not why he seemed compelled to be so surly. She suspected he would make it intolerable for any employee who arrived late or idled on the job and take satisfaction in doing so. But she was not one of his workmen and had no intention of allowing him to see that she was in any way alarmed by his aggressive rudeness.

Looking away from him, she began to gather up her sketches. "I didn't know the beach belonged to anyone," she said as she returned the papers to her straw bag. "You ought to put up signs."

"I'm not sure that would take care of the problem. People who don't bother to learn if they're appropriating other people's property would hardly be put off by signs."

Startled by his suspicion, which seemed totally out of proportion to the situation, her eyes slid up the lean, formidable length of him to the tanned, cynical face. Suddenly his broad shoulders seemed to fill the sky. He wore a tight, yellow knit shirt tucked into the snug waistband of his jeans, which rode low on his lean hips. His features had the sharp edges of an early cubist painting, the bronzed flesh taut over angular bones, and despite the hint of indolent sensuality in that wide mouth there was not the slightest suggestion of irresolution because she was a woman.

She got to her feet, clutching her bag to her side, and discovered to her chagrin that her knees felt a little weak. "There is certainly no need for you to be insulting," she said in a cool voice. "I haven't damaged your employer's property in the slightest degree. Nor do I see sitting on the beach as appropriating it."

The sound he made was filled with sarcastic disgruntlement. "Well, you're a cool customer, I'll give you that. But you college kids are all alike. You think the world is your oyster. I've already run off two bunches of you this week. The last ones had actually set up camp inside the hotel! When I informed them they were breaking the law and subject to arrest, they got very wide-eyed and innocent, too. Although I confess they weren't as articulate in their own defense as you are."

Aware of the fact that those insulting blue eyes were taking in every detail of her body in the damply clinging jumpsuit, she straightened the tie belt at her waist with a jerk.

"For your information, I've never camped out in my life. I have a room in a perfectly respectable hotel."

He smiled, mockery in his face. "Paid for by Daddy, I'm sure." His big, suntanned hands slid to the top of his low-slung jeans, the thumbs crooking over the waistband. "Daddy," he drawled, "should have taught you to respect other people's property."

Heat burned in her cheeks. She knew that she must look younger than her years, with no makeup and her hair tumbling into her face, and the knowledge made her feel at a disadvantage. The fact that he had called her "a cool customer," reminding her of Rob's accusation that she was cold and unfeeling, didn't help her temper, either. She had rarely found herself unable to appear calm and reasonable, even when she was feeling quite agitated inside. But this man and the ridiculous situation made her lose her composure momentarily,

"You're hardly in a position to criticize," she burst out, "since your own upbringing obviously lacked even rudimentary instruction in good manners. Are you always such an insufferable boor?"

"Just when confronted with trespassers—especially a saucy little coed who thinks she has only to wiggle her tail at a man to wrap him around her little finger." He shrugged, the trace of a cynical smile curving his lips, as if he got some kind of satisfaction from her emotional outburst. "That dewy-eyed come-hither look is wasted on me, I assure you."

Brook had never been so angry in her life. She looked at this insolent, golden-haired stranger with bitter revulsion and fury. "You're confused," she snapped. "If I should ever decide to issue the sort of invitation you're hinting at, it would certainly not be to the likes of you! Furthermore, I am not the sort of woman who—"

"Look." He cut her short impatiently. "I have work to do. I haven't time to play games. If you don't leave I'll have to resort to more drastic measures."

Her gray eyes flashed. "You would enjoy having me arrested, wouldn't you?"

He laughed humorlessly. "I don't think I'll need reinforcements." Sardonic challenge sparkled in his blue-black eyes.

She glared into his taunting face and knew he meant every word. "You'd like to use strong-arm tactics, I'm sure. I could hardly expect anything more civilized from such a caveman type."

She saw his jaw tighten, and then he said tersely, "If I've misjudged you, I apologize." But there was no apology in his look.

She gave him a glacial stare before she turned to walk away. She thought she heard a low-toned curse behind her, but she did not turn around. She gripped her fingers so tightly about the strap of her shoulder-bag that the nails bit into her palm. Her heart thudded in her ears, its increased tempo caused by temper and chagrin.

She pushed her falling hair off her damp forehead and hurried toward the bridge, her back rigid, her eyes seeing, as through a gauzy veil, the brilliant reflection of the morning sun in the water of the bay. For one second she had been tempted to slap the blond stranger's face or even to—what?

Ludicrous as it now seemed, she had actually considered flirting with him, leading him further into his already formed assumption that she found him attractive—and then, when he softened, giving him the brush-off. Instead, he had brushed her off!

She pressed her lips together, knowing that the uncharacteristic impulse to resort to such female strategies was nothing more than hurt pride wanting its revenge. He was nothing but an overdeveloped body and an ego to match. He wasn't worth her resorting to the cheap trickery that he obviously felt all females employed. She was glad now that she had maintained enough dignity to simply walk away.

By the time she reached the mainland again, her anger had been cooled by her natural common sense. She could even laugh a little over the fact that he had taken her for a college student. Fortunately he hadn't interrupted her before she'd made several good sketches of the pelicans.

Upon her arrival the day before, she had noticed an attractive little restaurant facing the beach about a half mile north of the Bridge of Lions. She decided to try it for breakfast and, after crossing the bridge, turned in that direction. Opposite the restaurant, as she was about to quit the beach and cross the street, a piping voice called out from near at hand.

"Hi!"

Brook turned around and saw a little girl of about six or seven wearing a green swimsuit, sitting spraddle-legged in the sand with the beginnings of a sand castle between her legs. Her bright blue eyes were looking directly into Brook's.

Something about the child touched a responsive chord in Brook. She turned back and strolled over to the bench beside which the child was sitting. "Hello," she said with a smile, seating herself on the bench.

"My name's Amanda. What's yours?"

"Brook." She glanced about. "Are you alone?"

Amanda swung her head around, causing the strands of her long brown hair to catch the sunlight and glimmer with golden highlights. "No. That's Rosa over there. She came with me."

Brook followed the child's gaze and saw a dark-skinned, middle-aged woman seated on another bench in the shade of a tree about twenty yards away. The woman, whose black hair was pulled back in a severe style, wore a plain gray dress and shining black shoes. She was watching Brook and Amanda with no expression except for a hint of watchfulness in the alert tilt of her head. Brook nodded in a friendly way, but there was no response from the dark woman.

"What are you building?" Brook asked.

"A castle," Amanda replied, "but the guard tower keeps falling down."

"Maybe you need a stick or something inside the tower to brace it." Brook got on her knees beside the little girl and, picking up a good-sized twig from the sand nearby, stuck it into the crumbling tower on one corner of the sand castle. "Now see if that will help."

Frowning with concentration, Amanda packed

19

more sand around the twig and chuckled happily when it did not crumble. "How did you know that would work?"

"I've built a few sand castles myself," Brook told her.

"I'm going to build a drawbridge and a moat and everything—like the fort over there." She pointed in the direction of the sprawling Castillo not far away, which had guarded St. Augustine from attack by sea when the Spanish held sway in the area. Amanda grinned at Brook, revealing a missing tooth in front and a dimple in one cheek. "I can't say its Spanish name, but Rosa can. Rosa speaks Spanish because she's from Mexico."

"The Castillo de San Marcos?"

Amanda's blue eyes widened. "Can you speak Spanish, too?"

"Not really," Brook confessed. "Only a few words." She glanced over her shoulder at the watchful, dark woman. "Is Rosa related to your family?"

"No." Amanda shrugged. "She's lived with us for years and years, though—since before I was born. She came to America to work because she could make more money here. She still has some brothers in Mexico. One of them is sick and Rosa sends him money."

Brook nodded her understanding, as Amanda began to scoop out a moat along one side of the sand castle. "Rosa cries about her brother sometimes." She looked up. "She's a good cook and she takes good care of me."

"Do you live in St. Augustine?" Brook asked.

"No. Daddy had to come here to do some work. I don't know how long we're going to stay." She looked up at Brook with a wistful expression. "Daddy is so busy I don't see him very much, and I

20

miss my friend Linda. Her house is across the street from mine at home."

From the corner of her eye, Brook saw the Mexican woman stand abruptly and walk toward them. Her dark eyes examined Brook with suspicious scrutiny before she said to Amanda, "Come, child, you have enough sun for this morning. We will go now."

Amanda glanced up, started to protest, but stopped mid-sentence and sighed. She got to her feet, knocking over the sand castle with one foot. "I'll build it later." She turned to Brook. "Will you be on the beach tomorrow morning?"

"Probably," Brook told her.

Amanda gave her another gap-toothed grin. "Good, then I'll look for you. Maybe you can help me build the castle."

"Good-bye, Amanda," Brook said as the child followed the solemn Rosa down the beach toward the bridge, her little shoulders drooping disconsolately. Brook could well imagine that Rosa provided little companionship for Amanda; she could not picture the Mexican woman playing with the little girl. Rosa did seem extremely protective, though.

Brook got up and, brushing the sand from her jumpsuit, crossed the street and entered the restaurant. A young, sandy-haired waitress approached her table as soon as she was seated. She placed a menu in front of Brook and eyeing her curiously asked, "Do you know the Darcys?"

Brook looked up from the menu. "Pardon?"

"The Darcys. I saw you with Amanda Darcy on the beach just now."

"Oh, Amanda." Brook smiled. "She's a charming little girl, isn't she? But I never saw her before this morning. I don't know her family."

21

"You must have heard of Dane Darcy, though."
The girl's look was quizzical.

"Dane Darcy," Brook repeated, thinking that the name did sound familiar and wondering where she had heard it before.

"Well, he's in the papers all the time," said the waitress, blinking her green eyes in emphasis. Whoever Dane Darcy was, the girl seemed incredibly impressed by him.

"The name does ring a bell," Brook admitted.

"He lives in Miami," the waitress confided. Then, seeing her employer eyeing her disapprovingly from behind the cash register, she hurried across the room and came back with a pot of coffee. "You do want coffee, don't you?" she asked, and when Brook nodded the girl filled her cup and gave Brook more gratuitous information about Dane Darcy. "He's so rich he probably doesn't even know how much he's worth. He's handsome, too. Women are always after him."

"I take it he isn't married," Brook murmured, feigning an interest in what the girl was saying while she perused the menu.

"His wife died," the waitress told her, "when Amanda was born. So he just buried himself in his work, you know, and got even richer."

Evidently Dane Darcy was Amanda's father. The waitress seemed to have created quite a drama in her mind, with the man in the starring role. Brook gave her order and sipped her coffee as she watched the girl retreat with obvious reluctance to the kitchen.

Yes, Brook was remembering now. She had heard of Dane Darcy—playboy, jet-setter, ruthless tycoon —he owned hotels and condominiums, and recently there had been a story in the newspapers about his alleged manipulation of the silver market. Brook had a fuzzy memory of the lean face in gray newsprint, the features unclear, but the willful arrogance recognizable. Poor Amanda—with only Rosa and Darcy for company! Brook felt a wave of sympathy for the child. Now that she thought about it, there had been something vulnerable in the little girl's eagerness to talk to Brook, a stranger, on the beach earlier. She must live a lonely life. Poor little rich girl. The cliché seemed definitely apropos in Amanda's case.

Chapter Two

Brook thought of Amanda Darcy several times during the remainder of the day, most of which she spent sketching interior and exterior views of the Castillo. Each time, with the memory came the dejected sight of the little girl leaving the beach in the Mexican woman's wake. Brook's sympathy for Amanda grew, and she made it a point to be on the beach the following morning.

Amanda found her only a few minutes after her arrival and, clearly delighted that Brook had remembered the place of their previous meeting, pressed her to help build a sand castle. Rosa hovered nearby, but she seemed a little less suspicious than the first day. She murmured her approval of the sand castle Amanda and Brook built, and, before the Mexican woman took her charge away, she said, "You are kind, señorita, to spend so much time with the child."

"I enjoy it," Brook told her and meant it.

During the remainder of the week, all of Brook's days started with meeting Amanda on the beach. She fell into the routine of sketching while Amanda played and chattered incessantly. It soon became evident that the little girl was bright and surprisingly unspoiled for a child who had been born to wealth; she worshipped her father, although Brook got the impression the man spent little time with his daughter.

On Friday, Brook's fifth day in St. Augustine, Amanda ran to meet her on the beach, bursting with good news.

"Guess what?" she greeted Brook. "Tomorrow's my birthday and Rosa is making a chocolate cake with candles and everything—and Daddy said I could invite you to dinner since you are my only friend here and—"

"Wait a minute—slow down!" Brook pleaded, laughing. She glanced at Rosa, who had followed Amanda to the spot at a much more sedate pace. The Mexican woman gave her the ghost of a smile and nodded.

"So," Brook said, tousling Amanda's long, silken hair, "tomorrow is your birthday, eh? How old will you be?"

"Seven," said Amanda. "We're having all my favorite foods—fried chicken and french fried potatoes and everything—and, oh please, say you'll come, Brook!"

"You're very sweet to want me," Brook told her, "but Amanda, I don't want to intrude on a family celebration."

Amanda darted a pleading glance at Rosa. "Tell her we want her to come."

"Señor Darcy has given his permission for Amanda to invite you," Rosa responded, although what Rosa's opinion in the matter was, it was impossible

25

to tell. She was the most unexpressive person Brook had ever met.

Amanda was jumping up and down. "Please, Brook! Say you'll come."

Brook laughed again, weakening in the face of the little girl's eagerness. "I don't even know where you're staying."

"On our boat," Amanda told her. "It's docked at the harbor by the bridge. It's white and the name's painted on it—Aphrodite. You must have seen it."

"Yes, I have," Brook admitted. It was clear that she was not going to be able to decline without breaking Amanda's heart.

"Could you come at seven-thirty, please?" Amanda persisted.

Overcoming her reluctance and even her better judgment, Brook finally said, "All right, I'll be there."

Later, after she had left Amanda, she was filled with misgivings. Brook had assumed the Darcys were staying in a hotel. She should have suspected, she supposed, that the only yacht in the harbor belonged to Dane Darcy.

She managed finally to brush her misgivings aside. She could, she decided, survive almost anything for a couple of hours—for Amanda's sake.

She spent Saturday morning finishing a watercolor of Amanda from sketches made during their time together on the beach. Late Saturday afternoon, she found a frame shop and had the painting matted, framed, and wrapped for Amanda's birthday gift.

After a quick shower, she wound herself in a towel and stood in front of the closet, surveying the sparse wardrobe she had brought with her to St. Augustine. What did one wear for dinner on a yacht?

Since she had brought mostly shorts and jeans,

there were only two dresses hanging in the closet. The more suitable one for dinner was a soft mauve silk cut to cling, but with a modest boat neck and full sleeves gathered onto elastic just above the elbows.

With the dress she wore bone leather sandals with narrow straps and heels. As she sat at the dressing table applying makeup and brushing her hair, she rather regretted that she hadn't bothered to pack any jewelry. But she doubted that anyone would take much notice of what she was wearing, anyway. Thank goodness. Now that seven-thirty was approaching, she wanted only to get to the yacht, stay there just long enough to satisfy Amanda, and come back to the hotel.

Dear heaven! she thought wryly as she left her room. How had she ever let herself be talked into this?

When she reached the bridge, she saw Amanda and a teenage boy dressed in jeans and a striped shirt—obviously a deckhand or cabin boy, or whatever one called servants on yachts. The two were standing on the dock and the young man, whose name Amanda said was Greg, helped her down a short ladder into the cockpit.

"We've been waiting for you," Amanda said, taking Brook's hand. The little girl wore a yellow cotton sundress with straps that tied at the shoulders, her hair pulled back and held in a ponytail with a yellow ribbon. Somehow she looked even more fragile to Brook than she did on the beach in her swimsuit.

Brook handed her the package she was carrying under one arm. "Happy birthday, Amanda."

Amanda's eyes sparkled. "Oh, thank you!" she breathed. Evidently a present was a present to a child, no matter how much money her father had.

"I'll open it. Come on." Amanda was practically dragging her toward a door that led into the large, many-windowed salon. It seemed to be something of an all-purpose area with a white leather sectional sofa and chairs piled with brown, beige, and tangerine throw pillows. The short draperies were printed with a geometrical design of beige, brown, and white. A round table and tangerine canvas deck chairs occupied one end of the area, with a few steps leading down to the galley and staterooms. It was really quite cozy and informal, not at all as luxurious as Brook had imagined, although in addition to being serviceable everything was obviously quite expensive.

A tall man was standing at the bar on the wall next to the galley stairs, his back to them. He put down his glass and turned slowly, pushing his hands into the pockets of his white jeans. His thighs were molded so tightly beneath the denim of the jeans that a ripple of hard muscle could be seen when he moved.

This registered only peripherally, however, for as he turned, Brook's glance took in the sun-bleached blond hair and the tanned, craggily chiseled face and her blood froze in her veins for one stunned second.

It was the foreman who had dismissed her from the construction site on Anastasia Island! Now—much too late—things were beginning to fit together. The hotel being built across the bay must be the "work" that had brought Amanda's father to St. Augustine. This rude, insufferable man worked for Dane Darcy!

Amanda, still clutching Brook's suddenly damp hand, led her deeper into the salon. "Daddy, this is my friend, Brook."

For a second Brook thought she was going to

faint. The blood left her head and she actually had to take hold of a chair to steady herself. It couldn't be! But it was. He didn't work for Darcy—he *was* Darcy!

It was no consolation at all to recognize the flash of surprise in the midnight-blue eyes and know that he was as disconcerted by this encounter as Brook herself.

She watched Dane Darcy cover the short distance between them with a litheness that was curiously graceful and reminiscent of some powerful jungle cat. His broad shoulders were emphasized by a black shirt open in front to reveal a mat of curling, blond chest hair.

Tension shot through Brook as he looked down into her face with a relaxed arrogance that shook her. If she had had even a glimmer of hope that he might not recognize her, it would have been dissipated by the hard black intensity of his gaze. No hint of a welcoming smile was offered to soften the chiseled firmness of his mouth.

As he towered over her, Brook suffered the raking scrutiny of his look, which seemed to take in every line of every feature—from her waving black hair and wide, gray eyes to the softly sculptured chin and smooth throat. It left Brook with the feeling that she was being analyzed bit by bit, with intense but dispassionate interest, like a set of blueprints.

"You are Amanda's friend, Miss—?" The timbre of his tone was low and totally controlled, like all the rest of him.

"Adamson." Somehow she got the word out, and then it was easier to add, "Brook Adamson, Mr. Darcy."

There was an insolent arching of one light-colored brow and a measured glitter of speculation in the dark depths of his look. "I believe we have met before." There was an underlying harshness now in the carefully modulated tones.

"Yes, on the island a few days ago." A stiff smile touched her lips. Had she obeyed the shouted command of every nerve in her body at that moment, she would have turned, run across the cockpit and left the yacht. Somehow she managed to stand her ground.

Her peripheral vision caught Amanda's ponytail bobbing beside her. "Look what she brought me, Daddy! May I open it now?"

Dane Darcy looked down at his daughter's eager, upturned face with an expression that indicated he had, for a moment, forgotten her presence. "Of course, princess. Go ahead."

Amanda ran to the couch, sat down, and began tearing into the package. Brook saw Rosa's dark form appear on the galley stairs. Over her gray dress, she wore a bibbed white apron.

"Señor Darcy," Rosa said quietly, her head tilted to one side and a questioning look on her face. "Shall I begin serving now?"

"In a few minutes. I must offer our guest a drink first." His eyes did not leave Brook's face as he spoke. "What would you like, Miss Adamson?"

"Nothing, thank you." Brook did not wish to prolong the evening's ordeal any longer than was absolutely necessary. At the same time, she did not want to give this man the satisfaction of watching her turn tail either. It was true there was a rather intimidating aura of command about Dane Darcy, but he had no authority over her.

He shrugged now, an eloquent dismissal of her refusal to accept a drink, and said to the Mexican woman, "We'll eat then, Rosa."

"Oh, Daddy, look!" Amanda had finally removed the wrappings from the portrait and was holding it up for her father's inspection. "Isn't it pretty? Brook is a good artist, isn't she?"

Dane Darcy took the watercolor from Amanda's hands and, after studying it for a moment, glanced at Brook with a knowing glint in his eyes. "Very good, princess. Thank you, Miss Adamson. We will enjoy looking at this. Shall we hang it in your stateroom until we get back home, Amanda?"

The child clapped her hands and agreed that this was a fine idea. "I'll hang it later," her father told her, laying the portrait on a table beside the couch. "Rosa has dinner ready now."

Brook followed the two of them to the table and took the chair Dane Darcy held for her. Only a few minutes earlier, she had been famished. Now, seated at the table and assailed by the delicious sight and smell of golden fried chicken, crisp french fried potatoes, a green bean casserole, and tossed green salad, her stomach contracted and she wondered how she would manage to swallow a bite.

Rosa served silently and efficiently, always remaining in the background, then retreated to the galley.

"I'm curious, Miss Adamson." Dane Darcy appeared maddeningly relaxed and, indeed, paused to add a generous topping of dressing to his salad. "Are you an art student?"

"I haven't been a student for four years," she informed him. "That is when I graduated from art school. I'm an illustrator. I'm in St. Augustine on an assignment."

"Am I to understand that if it were not for this assignment, my daughter and I would never have had the pleasure of meeting you?" He tipped his head sideways in challenge, his narrowed eyes not hiding the skepticism of his gaze. What did he mean by that look? She suspected that he was baiting her, but she had no idea why—or with what. She forced herself to meet his look. "That seems very likely," she agreed.

"I see. So we owe this pleasant little dinner to blind coincidence—fate, if you will."

"I don't know what you're getting at, but if you care to see this dinner as fated, go ahead." Hearing herself say the words, Brook realized that in some way she had risen to his veiled challenge, and the tone of her voice dared him to make something of it.

"I *don't* care to, Miss Adamson," Dane Darcy stated.

"Your meaning escapes me."

"*Does* it?" he inquired wryly.

"Daddy?" Amanda's puzzled voice caused Brook to become aware that the little girl sensed the tense undercurrent at the table and was totally confused by it. "What's wrong?"

"Nothing at all, Amanda." His gaze remained locked with Brook's.

Clearly not satisfied with that, Amanda persisted. "You sound like you're mad at Brook or something."

He tore his gaze from Brook's face and smiled at his daughter. "Now why would I be mad at her, honey? I don't even know her."

"She's my friend," Amanda stated with a stubborn thrust to her little chin.

Her father laughed. "And a very clever friend she is, too."

"Aren't you going to eat your dinner, Brook?" Amanda was gazing at Brook's untouched plate.

"Certainly I am," Brook assured her and, picking

32

up her fork, determined to eat at least some of the food if it choked her. This proved to be easier than she had expected, as long as she kept her glance scrupulously away from Dane Darcy, who continued to assess her while he ate with an attitude that Brook sensed was at least part displeasure. He really was the most obnoxious man she had ever met!

The meal seemed interminable to Brook and, she was sure, to Darcy as well. Amanda, however, kept up a stream of bright chatter that required only an occasional response from Brook or her father.

Eventually, Rosa brought in the birthday cake, and Dane Darcy rose to the occasion by starting to sing "Happy Birthday" in a deep, resonant voice. He watched Brook from beneath lowered lashes, his smug expression challenging her to join him. Since it would have puzzled Amanda even further if she had remained silent, Brook followed along with a smile fixed on her face for Amanda's benefit.

Then the little girl blew out the candles, and Rosa served the cake with ice cream.

Sighing, Amanda said happily, "Didn't I tell you Rosa was a good cook, Brook?"

"You did," Brook agreed and glanced at Rosa. "And you were right." The Mexican woman met Brook's look briefly and smiled before she left the room.

As they left the table after dessert, Brook was mentally planning how she would tell Amanda that she had to leave now. Before she could speak, however, Rosa appeared again and announced, "It's your bedtime, child."

The little girl put up a protest, but she was overruled by her father, who said she had had a long day and needed her rest. Looking crestfallen, Amanda kissed her father's cheek, extracted a promise from Brook to meet her on the beach the next morning, and followed Rosa from the salon.

Now was the time for Brook to excuse herself, but when she turned to Dane Darcy she found that he was standing in front of the door leading to the cockpit. She had the most ridiculous feeling that he was blocking her way.

"Thank you for dinner." She remained calm, although the determined set of his jaw revealed that he had something unpleasant on his mind.

He stared at her for a moment, then said abruptly, "Would you like that drink now?"

No, she wanted to yell at him. Yet she was curious about his reaction to her, which seemed, if possible, more strongly disapproving than when they had met on the beach. She wondered suddenly if she reminded him of someone whom he heartily disliked.

She heard herself saying coolly, "Yes, thank you," quite as if she had not vowed to leave the yacht as quickly as possible. As long as she was here, she told herself, she would stay long enough to find out if this man was capable of being civil. She might even discover why he had taken such a dislike to her.

He walked to the bar. "What would you like?"

"White wine." She moved to the couch and perched gingerly on the edge.

He brought her the wine, then stood looking down at her with the bowl of his brandy snifter cupped in one big hand. Brook realized now that it had been a mistake to sit down; it made her feel that she was in a subservient position. His dark eyes slowly swept over her from head to toe, missing nothing, lingering where the soft material of her dress shaped itself to her rounded breasts.

She drew herself up stiffly and raised the wine glass to her lips. It gave her something to do and then, because the silence seemed suddenly fraught with threatening tension, she said, "You have a charming daughter, Mr. Darcy."

"Rosa reports that you have been meeting Amanda every day on the beach." The words were clipped and hard, almost like an accusation.

"I've been spending a half hour or so with her each morning, yes. She seems lonely here without her friends, and I find our meetings delightful. Amanda is a very special little girl."

The corners of his firm mouth lifted cynically. "You are a woman who knows her way around the artistic community, and you expect me to believe you're delighted with the company of a seven-year-old child? I think not."

She shook her head, not trusting herself to reply for a moment, and slowly set her wine glass on the corner of a small table. She got quickly to her feet. "I stayed after dinner for only one reason—to see whether you knew the meaning of the word civility. Well, I have my answer. You are the most—"

"Insufferable, boorish caveman type lacking in rudimentary good manners. I believe that about covers it." He moved to lounge insolently in the doorway.

Her gray eyes were cool. "In a nutshell."

"I admit to a grudging admiration for the uniqueness of your approach, Miss Adamson. Insults— that's a new wrinkle. This thing with Amanda, of course, is old hat."

Her *approach*? A small inkling of the reason behind his churlishness came to her, and her mind whirled with shock. If he was insinuating what she thought he was . . . She took an audible breath. "I think you'd better explain what you mean by that."

He took a step toward her, his face suddenly hard with anger. "You are not the first woman to try to get at me through my daughter. The tactic is really not worthy of someone with your imaginative bent, Miss Adamson. Besides that, it was a low, conniving thing to do. Amanda really believes you're her friend."

She stared at him, incredulous disbelief sending trembling apprehension along all her veins. "You've misunderstood everything!"

Dane Darcy finished his drink and looked at her cynically. "That first morning at the construction site, you almost made me believe our meeting was accidental. I took you for a college kid."

"With a wiggling tail," Brook said bitingly.

His gaze, moving down over her body before returning to her flushed face, mocked her. "Yes, and you affected such injured innocence that I decided you really didn't recognize me or know whose property you were on. Even when Amanda started talking endlessly about her friend Brook, I didn't put it together. Not until you walked in here tonight."

"This is incredible." She tried to remain composed and not let his outrageous accusations tighten her voice. "I went to the construction site to sketch the pelicans. I hadn't the foggiest notion who you were when you put in an appearance. Of course, I had read in the papers of some of your 'exploits.' " She gave the word an unsavory ring. "But I didn't even know you were in St. Augustine until after I met Amanda, and never once did I suspect that you were her father. I—I thought you were a foreman. Believe me, if I had known the truth, I would never have come here tonight!"

He tilted his head and studied her with a look of dark amusement. "Impressive. Just the right ring of earnestness in the tone. You should have been an actress instead of an artist." He managed to dispose of the brandy snifter without moving away from the doorway. Then he placed his hands against either side of the door and stared at her with narrowed, glittering eyes.

Brook's feet somehow managed to carry her across the salon to face him furiously. "Get out of my way."

"Is that what you really want?" The lift of light brows italicized the mocking doubt in the voice. "Don't you intend to finish what you've started?" Nonchalantly, he raised a long finger, tucked it under her chin, lifted her face, and looked down into it with a calculating appraisal that suggested he was examining a mildly interesting bit of merchandise.

Instinctively, she took a step backward. "You make me sick!"

A wry smile quirked his mouth. "Sorry. I suppose it salves your conscience to pretend you came here only for Amanda's sake. It allows you to see yourself as the pursued instead of the pursuer." He chuckled humorlessly. "Forgive me, but I'm afraid I'm still capable of being taken aback by the paradox of the modern woman."

"Considering all the women who you claim throw themselves at you, I find that hard to believe." She smiled sweetly. "Surely your wide range of experiences must have exposed you to every approach by now."

"Touché," he mocked.

Brook glanced away from him, not letting him bait her into losing her temper. "I know your type, Darcy. The truth is you prefer your women submissive and worshipful and dependent on you for their identity. I've no doubt that if you had a wife you would want to keep her pregnant and barefoot." The words were out before she remembered that his wife had died in childbirth. An apology trembled on her tongue, but then she saw that she hadn't wounded him at all. He was impervious.

A flicker of wry humor sparked in the dark depths of his eyes. "Not an unattractive condition in a woman."

"The classic reaction of the male chauvinist!" She pushed aside her misplaced sympathy and was openly scornful. "I'm amazed that you have managed to be so successful in business when you are so boringly predictable!"

"Do you feel superior to all men?" he inquired with a curiously amused look.

"Not all men," Brook replied, "just certain types." She had already let Dane Darcy know what type she considered *him*. "If you will excuse me now, I have to go. My time is too valuable to waste any more of it here."

"Let me see," he mused tauntingly. "This is the hands-off scene, right? To set me up for the next time we meet when you will be, shall we say, more approachable? If you play your cards right, you can probably get Amanda to invite you here again."

A black rage clouded Brook's vision for a moment. "I would appreciate it if you would tell Amanda I won't be able to meet her tomorrow," she said through tight lips. "Say that I remembered another appointment. After meeting you, I realize that any further contact with your daughter is quite impossible."

"So that she won't be too disappointed," he drawled, "I'll try to spend the afternoon with her tomorrow."

"It's about time," Brook observed.

His mouth tightened. "I am a busy man. I've seen to it that Amanda is well cared for. She has nothing but the best of everything."

"Except her father."

He looked at her sharply. "I brought Amanda with me on this job so that we could have some time together in the evenings."

Brook smiled briefly. "When you can manage to elude your many female pursuers, which I am sure requires all of your considerable expertise. But surely you've exaggerated their number. There can't be all that many stupid women in the world."

She heard Dane Darcy inhale sharply. His eyes were like blue-black chips. "Is it because I saw through your little game? Is that why you are so determined to pretend you find me unattractive?"

"I am not pretending," she told him emphatically, raising her eyes to his face.

When he moved, it was so swiftly that Brook hadn't time to realize what was happening before she felt his hands gripping her shoulders and forcing her against his hard body. Her hands were crushed painfully against his chest, and his fingers wound themselves in her thick black hair, forcing her head back. His glittering eyes ravished her face and then his mouth came down slowly but surely, bruising her lips with uncaring force.

For a moment, she was stunned into limp passivity, but then awareness swept over her and she began to struggle fiercely, shoving against his chest, digging her nails into the thick blond mat of hair, fully intending to draw blood. She opened her mouth to insult him, but that was a mistake. He took advantage of her parted lips to explore her mouth more deeply with his tongue.

Then one hand disentangled itself from her hair to slide down her back to the curve of her hip and press her thighs against the hardness of his body. Brook was aware of a flare of arousal in the depths of her being. She felt invaded, violated, and gathering her senses at last, waited until the right moment, then bit down on his tongue.

He jerked back with an injured growl, releasing her. She backed away, shaking with reaction. "Keep your hands off me!" Her voice was thready and breathless. She made an effort to steady herself. "I don't know how someone like you managed to raise such a sweet child. It must have been Rosa's influence. I'm getting out of here, and I hope I never have to lay eyes on you again."

His eyes fixed on her face, he ran a finger slowly over the tip of his tongue.

"Let me pass! I—I'm going to scream my head off if you don't move away from that door," she said, her voice growing stronger.

He let his hand drop and gave her a wry grin. "No need. I found out what I wanted to know." He moved calmly aside.

Eyeing him warily, she slipped through the opening, then, breathing hard, scrambled across the cockpit and left the yacht, running.

When she reached her hotel room, she sank down on the bed without bothering to turn on a light. Moon glow filtered in through the loosely woven draperies at the glass doors that opened onto the balcony, silvering the room with a softly muted veil of unreality. She had left one of the glass doors partially open and a light breeze, heavy with the perfume of jasmine flowers, flowed around her, enveloping her in its heady fragrance that touched a nostalgic, melancholy chord in her.

Still breathing hard from the hurried return to the hotel, Brook touched a finger to the pulsing vein in her neck that betrayed the inner state of her nerves. She took several long, calming breaths to steady herself and began to feel a little quieter.

She had had to fend off men before, but never one as insultingly brazen as Dane Darcy. Never had she been so humiliated. He actually thought she had been pursuing him, using Amanda to get herself invited aboard his yacht! She hoped she had managed to disabuse him of that notion, but she wasn't sure that she had.

After a few moments, she undressed and, slipping a nightgown over her head, got into bed—on top of the sheets, for she felt hot. As the sweetly scented breeze caressed her body, she kept seeing those midnight-blue eyes, the way they had appraised every inch of her with such monumental arrogance. And she remembered the degrading response she had felt when Dane Darcy kissed her so ruthlessly.

Chapter Three

San Agustin Antiguo, the old town, Brook discovered, held the same fascination for her as it had the first time she ever saw it. During the next few days, after the debacle on Dane Darcy's yacht, she spent hours strolling along St. George Street, wandering through the quaint establishments—the blacksmith's, the silversmith's, the woodcarver's, the candlemaker's, the weaver's, the carefully restored houses dating from the Spanish colonial period—and filling her pad with sketches accurate to the minutest detail.

From the moment she stepped beyond the old city gate each morning, she could sense the past—a past that must have been filled with color and drama and, certainly, at times danger and disillusionment. But in retrospect that long-ago time seemed slow-paced and infinitely serene. Brook found the atmosphere oddly soothing and so she kept returning to St.

George Street and fell into the habit of ending each day there with a stop at the ice cream parlor.

It was on Thursday evening of the second week of her stay, as she was sitting at one of the small white tables in the ice cream parlor, dawdling over a dish of pineapple sherbet, that the serenity that she was beginning to take for granted was shattered. She had glanced sideways toward the door, but her mind was wandering and for a moment nothing registered. When it did, it was too late to pretend that she hadn't seen the newcomers.

Walking toward her table were Amanda Darcy and her father. Amanda saw Brook almost as soon as Brook had taken in the two and, with a whoop of childish delight, ran to her side.

"Brook! Where have you been? Why don't you come to the beach anymore?"

"I've been too busy." The excuse sounded lame even to Brook's ears.

The child's wide blue eyes were brightly accusing. "I thought you were my friend! Even when Daddy told me you couldn't come last Sunday, I looked for you on Monday and every day since."

"I—I'm sorry, Amanda," Brook stammered, feeling her cheeks flushing as Dane Darcy ran a comprehensive eye over her. She met his stare head on, chin held high.

"You forget that Miss Adamson is here to work, princess," he said, laying a big hand on his daughter's shoulder.

"Well, she doesn't work every minute! Do you, Brook?" Amanda demanded.

"No, honey, I have to eat and sleep, too," Brook told her, smiling, "but as I said, I've been very busy and I just haven't been able to spend much time on the beach." Her gaze had shifted to the child and she

43

scrupulously avoided letting it slide back to rest on the father's tan, chiseled face.

"There's a table open over there, Amanda," Dane Darcy said.

"Why can't we sit with Brook?" the child inquired with youthful imperviousness to nuances in the tone of adult voices. "You don't mind, do you, Brook?"

Brook shrugged helplessly. "Well—no, I guess not."

Amanda was already tugging at the chair next to Brook's. Dane Darcy hesitated only momentarily before taking the third chair.

"I still find it hard to believe that you're a successful illustrator, Miss Adamson," he said softly, to her surprise. "You don't look much older than Amanda in those shorts and halter." Then he picked up the menu and began to study it with apparent concentration, leaving her wondering if he had meant to insult her or to patronize her—or if he had meant anything at all.

While he and Amanda ordered, Brook played with her spoon, dipping it absently into the melting sherbet, her eyes on the gleaming white surface of the table.

"So," Dane Darcy said suddenly, "you no longer have time to idle away on the beach. I gather you believe in work before pleasure."

"On the contrary. My work gives me a great deal of pleasure."

"Nevertheless," Darcy retorted, "Amanda has found it difficult to accept that you could so easily forget all about her."

Brook's head lifted, the pale light picking out gleaming strands among the inky mass of her hair. The creamy skin covering her high cheekbones grew more flushed. "I haven't forgotten her," she told

44

him, bristling. "And she wouldn't be so dependent on strangers if you gave her more of your time."

He gazed at her from beneath half-closed lids. "For a woman who's had no experience in such things, you seem to know a lot about what my daughter needs." There was sarcasm in the words. "But you may spare me the lecture. Amanda and I have been together a great deal this week."

"Once we cooked dinner," Amanda informed Brook happily, "and gave Rosa the night off." She lifted blue eyes to her father's face. "Daddy, can Brook come and have dinner with us again? Tanya has eaten with us twice this week, but she isn't nearly as much fun as Brook."

Brook leaned forward to scoop up a spoonful of sherbet, and the narrowed blue-black eyes dropped to the thin material of her halter stretched across her full breasts, slowly probing the low neckline. Heat rose in her face, and his mouth curved suddenly in mockery. "You may have a point there, Amanda."

Angrily, Brook sat up, abandoning the melted sherbet and clenching her hands into fists. "I can't possibly have dinner with you again, Amanda. It's out of the question."

"Why?" The child's voice quavered upward.

A challenging glint sparked in Dane Darcy's eyes. "Yes, why, Miss Adamson?" he said softly, and her temper rose at the way he was baiting her in front of the child.

"As I said, I am working." She met Dane Darcy's insolent look and added deliberately, "But I am sure Tanya will be more than happy to fill in for me." Somehow she felt certain that Tanya was one of Darcy's women and from the surprised widening of his eyes she knew she had guessed correctly.

"Tanya's in love with Daddy, you know," Aman-

da announced with total unself-consciousness. "I
don't think he will marry her, though."

Dane Darcy laughed outright at his daughter's
audaciousness.

"I expect you are right," Brook said levelly,
looking at Amanda but intensely aware of Darcy's
unwavering regard.

"Apparently your friend Brook does not think
I'm the marrying kind," remarked Darcy, clearly
amused.

"What's the marrying kind?" asked Amanda,
frowning. "You were married to my mother, weren't
you, Daddy?"

"You know that I was, princess—a very long time
ago." His tone seemed subtly to have changed,
losing its light amusement and taking on a darkly
somber edge. "Eat your ice cream before it melts,"
he directed abruptly, turning his attention to the
sundae he had ordered.

"All right, Daddy," Amanda said obediently,
evidently subdued by the swift change in his manner.
She ate a few bites of her ice cream, then turned to
Brook. "You didn't say whether I'll see you on the
beach again—and you didn't say why you can't have
dinner with us."

Dane Darcy lifted his head, watching her. Brook
gave him a cold glance. "I can't make any promises,
Amanda. I'm here to make illustrations. Last week
when I came to see you on the beach in the
mornings, I wasn't as busy as I am now."

Amanda looked at her quizzically. "Don't you
want to have dinner with us again?"

"Amanda," Darcy said, his eyes narrowing on
Brook's face, "don't badger Miss Adamson. Maybe
the evening she spent on the yacht did not come up
to her expectations. I think she might be afraid to
come."

"I am not the least bit afraid," she snapped. "It would be more accurate to say that my time here is limited and can be spent to better advantage in other places."

His mouth crooked cynically. "And you are a woman who weighs the advantages, aren't you?"

She pushed her dish away, preparing to rise. "I really can't stay here any longer." She hesitated, seeing the crestfallen look on Amanda's face. "If I happen to be near the beach any morning soon, I'll look for you, Amanda." She fumbled for her check, which was tucked under her ice cream dish. "Good evening."

Darcy, who had been watching her with an unreadable expression, half rose now, gripping her wrist. "Sit down, Miss Adamson. I'll give you a ride back to your hotel."

Surprised by the command, she unwillingly sank back into her chair. Amanda was watching them with wide eyes, plainly confused by what was taking place. Brook had no wish to frighten her, nor to create a scene in a public place. Dane Darcy held her gaze for a long moment, then released her and leaned back. "Do you want the rest of your ice cream, princess?" he asked as coolly as though nothing had happened.

Amanda finished eating, and her father summoned the waitress and paid the bill for the three of them. They left the ice cream parlor and walked the two blocks toward where Darcy had left the Cadillac he had rented for his stay in St. Augustine. He strode beside Brook with Amanda hanging onto his hand. Reaching the black car, he opened the passenger door, and Amanda scrambled into the center of the front seat. Darcy waited for Brook to get in, then walked around to slide in under the wheel.

"I'm staying at the Monterey," Brook said.

47

"I know," he said curtly without elaboration and started the motor, turning to look over his shoulder as he backed the car.

By the time they had traveled a few blocks, Amanda's head was resting against Brook's arm. She yawned broadly.

"Hey, sleepyhead," Brook said lightly, "what did you do today that made you so tired?"

"We walked and walked," Amanda murmured drowsily. "We saw the old jail—and the mill—oh, and I forget what else." She snuggled closer to Brook, closed her eyes, and was soon breathing deeply.

"I knew she would be dead to the world as soon as we started driving," Darcy remarked without inflection.

Brook stared down at the child for a moment. "Now that Amanda is asleep, there is no need for you to make conversation. In fact, if you will stop the car, I'll find a taxi."

"Don't be ridiculous," he retorted, glancing toward her, his light brows drawn over the blue-black eyes in an impatient frown. "You can't seriously think I mean you any harm."

Brook sighed. "No, but you needn't pretend we have anything to talk about, either."

He braked the car at a light, his eyes brooding on the traffic. She stared straight ahead, embarrassingly aware of the man's sun-bleached hair carelessly falling across his forehead, the bronze profile, and the broad shoulders in the sky-blue ribbed knit shirt. "Strange as it may seem to you, I don't enjoy your company any more than you enjoy mine. I wouldn't have consented to your driving me if I hadn't been forced to agree—or make a fuss in front of Amanda."

There was a silence. She turned her head and

found him eyeing her with an odd expression. He pressed down on the accelerator and the car purred away from the intersection. At the next corner, he swung onto the road that led to the coast highway.

"There's a shorter way to the Monterey," Brook told him quickly.

"I am aware of that," said the dry, cynical voice. "I want to talk to you, Brook."

"I prefer Miss Adamson," she said stiffly.

"Surely we needn't be formal." He sounded sardonic.

"Mr. Darcy, I—"

"Dane," he said flatly.

"Dane, then," she said. "I am tired and I would like to go back to my hotel."

"Don't raise your voice or you'll wake Amanda," he commented mildly. "How long do you plan to stay in St. Augustine?"

"Until my work is finished," she responded tersely. "I can't give you an exact number of days. I'm not at all sure I would, even if I could, since it is none of your business."

He was seemingly unperturbed by the sharp rejoinder. "So you enjoy it—your work, I mean."

"Yes," she said grudgingly.

"Do you make a living at it?" He sounded interested.

"I've only been able to work at illustrating full time during the last ten months. Before that I worked for an ad agency and did free-lance jobs at night."

"You are ambitious."

There was no particular intonation in the statement, but she sensed a challenge nevertheless. "I imagine you disapprove of ambition in women."

He laughed outright at that. "Why would you think that?"

"Your kind usually does," she said.

His eyes slid over her face briefly before he returned his attention to the road. "Oh, yes, I remember. That night on the yacht you called me a chauvinist, an assessment you made on the basis of virtually no evidence. I hate to knock your neat little label into a cocked hat, but I happen to admire women who have successful careers. They don't have to depend on someone else for their self-esteem."

She flushed. "Some *man,* you mean?"

He shrugged. "It happens frequently." There was a peculiarly bitter edge to the words that reminded her of that moment in the ice cream parlor when he had spoken of Amanda's mother. She wondered suddenly what sort of person his wife had been. What had that young waitress said? That Amanda's mother had died when the child was born—and that Dane Darcy had then buried himself in his work. She found it difficult to imagine the man beside her as a devoted husband, but it was possible that his wife's death had changed him. In spite of his reportedly varied amorous exploits, he seemed almost totally self-contained to Brook, as if tender emotions were never allowed to surface—except perhaps with his daughter. She wondered if he were lonely. What was that old cliche? Alone in a crowd.

Brook shook her head slightly, disconcerted at the direction of her thoughts. Dane Darcy was the last man on earth who seemed capable of a love so deep that he still carried the scars after seven years.

"Have you ever been married?" he asked suddenly, jolting her from her reverie.

"No."

"Any boyfriends?"

"Nobody important," she replied tonelessly and then sighed with relief as she saw her hotel come into view.

"Why is that?" He seemed to be surprised at her answer.

"You mean, why don't I have a relationship with a man?" she asked with sarcasm. "How can I *live* without a man?"

"It seems a shameful waste, that's all." He grinned wickedly.

"I imagine I am supposed to take that as a compliment and feel enormously flattered." She met his taunting eyes without wavering. Dane Darcy was a man who manipulated women—and used them ruthlessly. He took what he wanted from them without a thought of what they might be feeling, of what damage might be done to them emotionally. His view of women was plain enough from what he himself had said to her and the way he had treated her that night on his yacht. Brook's independent spirit and moral fiber rebelled against such a man.

She had no idea what these personal questions were in aid of, but she had no intention of becoming a casual plaything for this man's amusement. Yet she was nervously aware of some primitive chord in her that quivered every time she set eyes on him. Something in her was drawn to him. Her integrity demanded that she avoid Dane Darcy like the plague.

The Cadillac slid into the hotel parking area and came to a smooth stop. Brook turned to ease Amanda's head, which was still pressed against her arm, back against the cushioned seat. While she was doing this, Darcy got out of the car and came around to open her door.

She stepped out, brushing past him. "Thanks for the lift."

He gripped her arm and walked beside her. "Where is your room?"

"On the second level. You needn't come with me."

He made a gruff sound and continued to walk beside her. When they had reached the stairs leading to the second level, he released her arm, but he moved in front of her, effectively blocking her way.

"Why are you refusing to see Amanda?"

Brook watched uneasily as he lounged in the doorway. The blue-black eyes were unreadable. She gave him an irritated look. "I regret not seeing Amanda but, under the circumstances, I really have no choice."

"Not true," he remarked in clipped tones. "There is always a choice."

"Well then, I choose not to see Amanda because I think it's best for everyone."

"It isn't what's best for Amanda," he contradicted her, "and you know it."

She shrugged, but the look in his eyes made her tense. "I don't like being accused of having an ulterior motive for befriending your daughter. And since you are determined to draw all the wrong conclusions about me—" Her voice trailed off uncertainly.

His eyes ran slowly, appreciatively over her, lingering on the quickening pulse in her throat. His hand moved lightly up her arm. "If I'm wrong," he drawled, "why *did* you spend so much time with Amanda at first?"

She was not unused to being noticed by men, but Dane Darcy was a master of the art. The insolent appraisal was insulting, but it nevertheless sent a trembling awareness through her that was unlike anything she had experienced before.

She was finding it difficult to take enough air into her lungs, which left her feeling breathless, and that made her angry. Lifting her chin defiantly, she

52

retorted, "Let's just say it was my maternal instinct."

His lopsided grin was derisive. "I've yet to meet a woman who looks like you, Brook, who has any maternal feelings whatsoever." His eyes looked black now as they rested with glittering intensity on her face, and his fingers tightened on her arm. He stared at her mouth until she was shaking.

"Well, there is a first time for everything," she breathed, surprised at the weak sound of her own voice.

A finger of his free hand touched her hot cheek. "You're an extremely desirable woman," he observed laconically, "and you are very well aware of it."

His hand slid behind her head, cradling it, the strong fingers entangled in her hair. She was aware that the blond head was moving downward and she stared, as if she were mesmerized, at his mouth. Involuntarily, her own lips parted slightly and lifted.

It seemed an eternity until the contact was made and then she lost all thought of propriety as her senses flared crazily, spinning in a whirlwind of feeling. Her arms went around his neck; her body arched against him as his mouth plundered hers in a kiss more provocative and intimate than any she had ever known.

Time spun out and finally his mouth left hers to seek out the sensitive skin of her throat in a hot exploration that forced an involuntary moan from her lips. Her head fell back, giving him further access. Nor could she make any effort to halt the hand that pushed her halter aside and moved freely, caressing her breast. She had never allowed any man such intimate access to her body before, but the honeyed tenderness he was arousing in her dazed her and left her weak and without a will of her own. She was only vaguely aware that her fingers were stroking the back of his neck and moving over his back, driven by a compulsive need to touch him, to become familiar with the contours of his body.

The descent of his mouth to the tender ripeness of her breast sent a shudder of arousal through her. He groaned, a thick, guttural sound, and lifted his head to look into her flushed face. Becoming slowly aware of his gaze burning over her features, she opened her eyes reluctantly and was dazzled by the black fire in his eyes.

She blinked in confusion and bewilderment, her senses still throbbing from his assault. His head was tilted slightly above her, the light from the stairwell giving the outline a golden haloed effect. The sensuous mouth that had dominated and shaken her emotions to their depths was hard with arrogant satisfaction.

"Tell me more about that maternal instinct," he said, his mouth curving in amusement.

"What—?" she breathed, trying to take in what he was saying. "I—I don't have to explain myself to you."

He grinned at her. "No explanation is needed." His fingers moved warmly against her nape. "You're a devastatingly sexy woman, and I'm clearly not the first man to discover it."

She was trying desperately to gather her thoughts into some semblance of order. Contrary to what he obviously believed, he was the first man ever to have such a profound effect on her. She wondered how he would feel if he knew Rob McAnnally had said she was cold and unfeeling, not even a woman. She stared into the hard, jaded face and knew she was completely in over her head with him.

She moved suddenly out of his arms and gripped the iron banister of the stairway for support. "You are bent on painting me in an uncomplimentary light, no matter what I say."

The dark eyes surveyed her with such calculated cynicism that the hot surging of her senses he had caused was abruptly stilled, and she felt chilled.

"I am perfectly willing to have you paint me a truer picture, Brook," he said lazily. "Now—or whenever you say."

Her mouth felt dry, her lips stiff and bloodless. "No, thanks. I've spent more time with you already than I care to."

"Could it be that you are afraid to see me again?" He stared into her eyes for a moment, then took a step toward her, a movement that cleared the stairway enough for her to brush past him. She whirled and ran up the stairs, driven by a desperate need to put distance between them. Her hand shook as it closed over her key, which she rammed into the lock, turning it viciously. She shoved open the door and stumbled into her room.

She leaned back against the closed door, gasping with the effort to draw enough oxygen into her body. For several moments her heart continued to pump thunderously in her ears. When the rhythm slowed, she kicked off her sandals and, without turning on the light, walked across the thick carpet to stare at the shadowy reflection of herself in the dresser mirror.

She felt as if she were looking at a stranger. Her hair was disheveled, her eyelids heavy, her mouth swollen and still tender from Dane Darcy's relentless assault. For a long moment she watched the rise and fall of her breasts beneath the thin cotton of her halter.

Then abruptly she turned away and lay down across the bed, staring into the dusky shadows in the corner of the room. How could it be possible that the most irritating, insulting man she had ever known could make her so aware of his intense masculinity that her pulses raced merely at the thought of him? His presence had such a catastrophic effect on her senses that she forgot all about her pride or integrity.

If she had had any doubt before about the wisdom of seeing Amanda again, it was effectively removed. She had to avoid anyone even remotely connected to Dane Darcy. She had to protect her foolish emotions against any possible avenue of approach.

Chapter Four

During the next few days, Brook threw herself into her work with intense determination. The beauty and romance of St. Augustine had been seriously dimmed for her by Dane Darcy. This gave her one more thing for which to resent him, and she now wanted to finish the assignment as quickly as possible and leave the old town behind. She would return at another time, she told herself, when she could appreciate it again.

One evening Lloyd Pennington, the author of the St. Augustine book, phoned her hotel room.

"How are the illustrations going?"

It was good to hear his friendly voice. "Very well, Lloyd. There are so many possibilities here. I hope you'll like the work I've done. At any rate, I'll have a stack of sketches for you to choose from."

He chuckled. "I can hear the excitement in your voice, so I know you're satisfied with what you've done. I was a little afraid you might be finding full-time illustrating too much of a good thing." She realized he was speaking from his own experience. When she had worked with him before, he had told her he'd tried full-time writing, but decided he preferred teaching English in a small college and writing only part-time.

"I doubt that I'll ever feel that way," she told him. "I've never been more content with my work in my life. It's exactly what I've always wanted to do."

"Do I detect a note of reservation?"

Puzzled, she asked, "What do you mean?"

"You were very careful to say you are content with your *work*. What about the other areas of your life?"

She responded lightly, "You just can't help playing father, can you? By the way, how are the children and Kim?"

"Everybody's fine. Kim's pregnant again."

"My goodness!" Brook laughed. "This will make five, won't it? You two are really serious about this family thing, aren't you?"

"Well, I don't think Kim's as serious as she used to be," he replied with amusement. "She informs me there won't be a sixth."

"When's the new arrival due?"

"Oh, not for five months yet. It takes almost as long as giving birth to a book. But I've about finished the rewrites and I'm considering coming to St. Augustine for a couple of days—just to make sure we're on the same wave length on the illustrations."

"Don't you trust me?"

"Sure I do. Only you know how I am. I have to have my nose in everything."

"I remember," she told him, smiling.

"Since summer vacation is coming up at the college, it would be a good time. I'm trying to talk

Kim into coming with me, but she's expecting her mother for a visit and feels it would be too much of an imposition to ask her to baby-sit while the two of us go off on holiday. I'm still working on her, though."

"Listen, Lloyd," Brook said seriously, "I had hoped to be finished here in another week or two. So you'd better check with me again before you come."

"What's your hurry?" he inquired. "I thought you loved St. Augustine."

"I do, but I can't idle away too much time—not since I'm depending wholly on free-lance work for my living."

"Okay. I'll decide definitely if and when—and soon. I'll let you know. Take care."

Brook hung up, wishing that she *could* dawdle away another month on this assignment, and it wasn't only finances that stopped her. If she stayed that long, she would be certain to run into the Darcys again. This was a small town. She reflected once more how Dane Darcy had barged in and disrupted her life, and she resented it enormously.

She spent most of the next day in her room, going through her sketches and jotting down ideas for a book cover. She wanted to have several scenes in color for Lloyd Pennington and the publisher to choose from. She kept coming back to the pelican sketches and, finally, did a rough drawing of several of the birds with the Castillo in the background. She became so engrossed that she forgot about lunch until after five.

When she glanced at her watch and saw how late it was, she realized that she was quite hungry. She put her work aside and got up from her chair to stretch her cramped muscles. She decided to shower and change, then walk along the beach until she saw a restaurant that appealed to her for dinner.

A half hour later, she emerged from the bathroom and dressed in cool white slacks and tunic and white sandals with spike heels. As she sat at the dressing table to brush her hair and apply makeup, she noticed that being out of doors so much during the past two weeks had given her a golden tan that appeared even darker in contrast with the white of her clothing. Another of the advantages of illustrating, she told herself—she could acquire a tan while working.

She felt happier than she had in days and began humming to herself as she went in search of her white clutch purse. She found it on the top shelf of the closet and switched her room key and coin purse containing bills as well as coins from the straw bag that she had been using for every day. She was checking the contents again to make sure she hadn't forgotten anything when there was a knock at the door.

She opened it to find Dane Darcy lounging in the hallway. "Hello, Brook."

She stiffened. "What are you doing here?"

He gave her a wry grin. "You haven't had dinner, have you?" His eyes ran over her white tunic and slacks and the purse clutched in one hand.

"What do you want?" she said warily.

"Will you have dinner with me?"

Brook was puzzled and suspicious as she looked up at him. In a tan linen suit worn with a dark aqua silk shirt open at the throat, he was as devastatingly handsome as she remembered. But she didn't trust him an inch. "That's a very bad idea," she said bluntly.

"Why?"

"Because I know you have to have some ulterior motive. I just don't know what it is—and I don't want to know."

"You've got me wrong, Brook," he murmured with a dry smile. "I'm not up to anything underhanded. It's merely that I've thought about you frequently since our last meeting, and I'm still puzzled. I've never been able to live with unanswered questions, and you're an enigma that I want to figure out."

"I don't believe you. I've been perfectly honest and straightforward with you. There's nothing to figure out."

"Have you tried the Chart House? I've reserved a table there."

"I suppose you thought I couldn't possibly say no!"

He shrugged. "I'll use the table—with or without you. I'd much prefer that it be *with* you. If you've eaten there, you know how good the food is."

"The Chart House is a little rich for my pocketbook," Brook said impatiently, "and I doubt that I'm dressed for such elegant surroundings so—"

He cut her off. "You look perfectly fine to me. Lovely, in fact."

"Dane," she said, her exasperation making her tone brittle, "I've been working hard all day—that is why I'm here, after all—and I'm tired and hungry. I don't feel up to bandying words with you. So if you will excuse me, I'll go about my business."

"I'd like to talk to you about my daughter."

"Amanda is the one you should be taking to dinner," Brook retorted. "If you had started to worry about her sooner, you wouldn't be wanting to talk to a stranger about her now."

The dark blue eyes were intent on her. "Did you ever really care one whit for Amanda?"

"I think I've already answered that question."

"What did you hope to accomplish by befriending her?"

"I didn't hope to accomplish anything," Brook snapped. She gave him an angry glare. "Do you know, you're the most pigheaded man I've ever met. You can't believe that anyone does anything for purely unselfish reasons—or even for no reason at all. It's beyond your comprehension that Amanda and I could merely like each other."

"If you like her so much, you'll come to dinner with me," he challenged.

For a moment, she just stood there wondering if she was insane to even consider going out with him, then she sighed and, stepping across the threshold, pulled the door shut behind her.

Outside, he helped her into the long, black Cadillac. The plush, white leather interior of the car smelled faintly of the citrus after-shave that Dane Darcy wore. When he started the engine, it purred so softly that she could barely hear it. He glanced at her as he put the car into gear and gave her a smile that struck her as a deliberate attempt to charm her. He had very potent weapons, she thought tiredly.

"That white looks great with your tan."

Brook cast him a doubtful look. "Why this sudden need to talk about Amanda?"

"Let's wait until we reach the restaurant, shall we?" he said calmly, steering the car expertly into the traffic. Brook leaned back in the comfortable seat, wondering what she had gotten herself into. Dane switched on soft music, and they made the short drive to the Chart House in silence.

To her vexation, she was potently aware of the long, muscular body beside her—of the strong hands that were curved around the steering wheel, of the masculine angles of his profile and the thick, gold lashes fringing the dark eyes, even of the heady aroma of after-shave mixed with the faint smell of clean male flesh. He might be hateful and arrogantly cocksure, but he was an exciting man, and one she found it impossible to ignore. How could she ignore him when he was having such an effect on her senses?

The restaurant was a converted family dwelling, one of those grand old Spanish-style houses that had been built fairly early in the town's history. Inside, the lighting was dimly intimate, but there was enough light to illuminate the high, beamed ceilings and the beautiful tiled floor. Their table overlooked a lighted courtyard, a lush vista of green shrubbery and manicured lawn, flamboyant flowers in red and pink and yellow, and narrow curving walks.

When they had ordered, Brook sipped her wine and nervously fingered her silverware. "What did you want to say about Amanda?"

His head tilted, the light picking out golden glints in the thick, waving strands of his hair. "I'm worried about her," he said seriously.

She gazed at him from beneath dark lashes. "Why?"

He shifted in his chair. "She's always been happy and well-adjusted, but ever since that night you were on the yacht, she hasn't been the same. She's cranky and short with Rosa. That's totally unlike her. And at times she's withdrawn, especially since we saw you in the ice cream parlor. I've been spending more time with her than usual, but it hasn't helped."

"Maybe you just never noticed before." Brook leaned forward to emphasize her point. "Maybe it's *because* you're spending more time with her now that you've seen what was there all the time. I can't believe Amanda has been totally happy without a mother and seeing so little of her father all these years."

63

"You're wrong. I haven't been as indifferent to my daughter as you seem to think. She's changed, and you're the reason."

Brook sat straight again, surveying him with irritation. "So if Amanda is unhappy, it's someone else's fault. You couldn't be to blame."

"Yesterday she accused me of making you stay away from her."

"Amanda is a bright child."

"But I haven't made you. Quite the opposite."

"Oh, maybe you believe that, but we both know why I don't feel that I can see Amanda anymore."

Their first course arrived, and she occupied herself with that, her head bent, ignoring the scrutinizing gaze that he had fixed on her. "What is it you're really after, I wonder," he murmured and she looked up at him angrily. "Some kind of trade-off, perhaps? What do you want in exchange for resuming your friendship with my daughter?"

Defiantly, she picked up her fork and speared a sliver of tomato from her salad bowl. "I suppose you're determined to find something so that you can stop bothering with her and get back to what you really want to do? It must be frustrating for you to have a problem that money can't solve."

"I have found there are very few problems that enough money won't take care of," he remarked over his salad.

She lifted her head. "What Amanda needs is not a paid companion. She's a lonely child who is unsure of her father's love."

Dane Darcy's mouth crooked in a scornful smile. "That's ridiculous. I'm beginning to think that Amanda's real problem is that I've spoiled her. I would not have made the same mistake with a son, but I've tended to feel that females are for pampering. Now, it appears, I am to pay for seeing that she's had everything she wanted. She doesn't appreciate her good fortune."

She shook her head in disbelief. "You sound like some aristocrat out of the nineteenth century. Females are for pampering! I've heard nonsense from men like you before, but that takes the cake!" Her tone was cutting. "Females are human beings. Little girls need the same things that little boys need."

His eyes sparked with dry amusement. "Did you tell Amanda that her father doesn't understand her? Did you tell her that I had forbidden you to see her?"

Brook gave him a cold glance. "No, although I hardly expect you to believe that."

He inclined his blond head, his midnight-blue eyes narrowing. "I am still reserving judgment, Brook. You're an intelligent and shrewd woman. Incredibly, within the space of a week, you managed to worm your way into my daughter's affection to the extent that she felt abandoned when you put a stop to your meetings with her. When did you discover that Amanda was my daughter?"

"Why do you keep asking me the same questions? I told you that night on the yacht that I learned her name the first day I ever saw her. But I had only a vague notion of who her father was—and I certainly never made the connection between Amanda's father and you until I boarded the Aphrodite."

Their fillets arrived and as he cut into his he said, "I am always suspicious of coincidences."

Brook responded hotly. "You are suspicious of *everything*, Dane Darcy!" She looked down at her fillet for a moment and then pushed her plate away. "I think I've lost my appetite, and this conversation doesn't seem to be going anywhere. If you will excuse me—'' She fumbled beside her chair for her purse, preparing to rise.

He stared at her. "Eat your dinner, Brook. I don't want my steak to get cold while I have to go chasing after you."

Knowing that he would do just that, she remained seated, fuming inwardly. He continued to eat his dinner as coolly as though they were the best of friends. Eventually, she ate too.

Over their coffee, she made one final attempt to make him see the problem as she saw it. "Amanda feels insecure. Spoiling a child isn't the same thing as showing her love. That takes much more time and effort. Have you thought about leaving your work for the summer and just being a father to your daughter? Do things with her, talk to her. That's what she needs—her father showing that he cares for her. The only reason Amanda is drawn to me is that she doesn't get enough of your time and attention."

He did not reply for several moments. His expression was difficult to discern, the light brows drawn over the dark eyes in a deep frown. It wasn't until he spoke that she realized he was angry. "I won't let Amanda grow up dependent and clinging. She has to learn to stand on her own two feet—for her own good."

Brook's eyes widened as she stared at him. It was not the first time he had expressed an aversion to clinging females and, as before, she wondered what was behind such a strong feeling. "For heaven's sake, Dane," she exclaimed. "Amanda is seven years old!"

"I am aware," he replied tersely, "of my daughter's age. I am also aware that the child is mother of the woman." He frowned slightly, his eyes holding her gaze for a long moment. "Do you seriously think my taking the summer off would make the situation better?"

Brook nodded. "Oh, yes."

He laughed softly. "You really do seem concerned about her."

"I *am* concerned," she said urgently. "You must surely know that Amanda is extremely bright, and bright children are often more vulnerable and sensitive than others."

"Better at manipulating their parents, too," he observed dryly.

Before she could reply, he summoned the waiter and paid the bill. Out on the narrow sidewalk, he didn't speak again as he strode beside her. In the car, he didn't immediately start the engine, but turned to her with an odd expression. "Will you answer one more question honestly?" She wondered if this meant he had decided she really had been acting out of simple interest in Amanda when she furthered the friendship during that first week. But she had no idea if that were the case or not. It was difficult to fathom what was going on behind that handsomely chiseled face.

"I'll try," she replied cautiously.

"Do you really find me unattractive?"

She managed a wry laugh. "I'll tell you what I told you before because it's the truth. You are obviously physically attractive, but you're not a man I could be seriously interested in. And *I'm* not a woman who takes up trivial relationships with men."

She thought he had decided to believe her, for he started the engine and drove directly to her hotel without responding. He found an empty parking space in the hotel parking lot and cut the engine.

When she saw that he was going to get out, she said nervously, "Thank you for dinner. You needn't come up."

"I thought we settled that the last time I brought you home." He got out and went around the car to open her door.

Standing in the hall outside her room, she fumbled in her purse for her key. When she found it, he took it from her hand and unlocked the door, following her inside.

Brook felt a flush creeping up her neck. "I'd prefer that you not come in. I'm very tired and I'd like to get to bed early."

His mouth crooked cynically. "I'm already in." He strolled about the room, glancing at the furnishings as if he were considering renting the room himself. "Why are you so nervous?" he inquired as he came back to stand in front of her. "You aren't going to pretend I'm the first man ever to enter your bedroom, are you?"

His mocking tone and the arrogant manner with which he was looking at her filled her with instant rage, and she reacted without thinking. She slapped his face with all her strength. His head jerked back, and he reacted by grabbing her arms, pinning them at her sides. They stared into each other's eyes for a long moment, both breathing heavily.

Then he crushed her against him and his mouth assaulted hers in a plundering kiss. She struggled futilely in the iron grip of his arms. But her struggles were only causing him to hold her tighter and, realizing this, she let her body go limp against him.

He evidently took this as surrender on her part, for his grip became less hard and more caressing. His hands ranged downward to her hips, pulling them against his own. His kiss softened, became more seductively sensuous.

68

In spite of her resolve, Brook's betraying body was invaded by liquid fire that began in the pit of her stomach and spread quickly through every vein.

His head lifted and he looked into her flushed face with glazed eyes. "I wanted to kiss you like this that first day." He bent to brush aside the material at the V neck of her tunic and found the hollow between her breasts. "You have a beautiful body—your skin is like silk. You really don't want me to go, do you?"

His invading lips trailed to the soft upward curve bared by the disarrangement of her tunic. The exquisite torture of his exploring mouth caused her to tremble, betraying the response that she was fighting, with growing desperation, to hide.

"Stop, Dane," she groaned.

"Admit it, Brook," he muttered thickly. "You want me to stay, don't you?"

"No," she gasped out breathlessly.

He lifted his head and looked at her with a mocking smile. "You're a liar." His tongue traced her lips, bringing more heat to her pulsing blood. "Be honest with me for once," he continued in a taunting tone. "Tell me what you really want me to do. Say it."

"I—I want you to leave at once."

He gave her another mocking smile and captured her lips to continue his bittersweet invasion. Furious at his arrogant assumptions, determined to maintain her pride at all costs, Brook somehow managed to keep her mouth firmly shut and remain impassive and unresponsive in his arms. At last, he stopped trying to force a response from her and lifted his head. As his arms released their hold, she almost stumbled with faintness and relief. But humiliation gave her some strength and she pulled away from him, stooping to pick up the purse that she had dropped when he grabbed her.

"You—you had no right to do that." Her whole body shook now with indignation that was not entirely aimed at him. "I feel sorry for Amanda, having a father like you!"

"Do you?" Dane's dark eyes glinted across the space she had put between them. She thought she detected a trace of regret in his expression, but when he spoke his words were harsh. "Time will tell how concerned you are about Amanda," he bit out. "If you care anything for her, you'll resume your meetings on the beach."

"Get out of my room—out of my life!" she said bitterly.

He regarded her through heavy gold lashes that shrouded his expression in mystery. Then he inclined his head. "Good night, Brook." He strode from the room without a backward glance.

As tired as she was, it took a long time for Brook to get to sleep that night. Her mind kept playing back everything that had happened with Dane, everything that he had said to her. She thought about Amanda, knowing that her father was oblivious to the child's real needs. Even realizing as she did that Dane's final challenge, flung at her before he left, was tantamount to emotional blackmail, she couldn't bring herself to continue making Amanda pay for her father's arrogance. No ordinary child would have placed such importance on a brief friendship with an adult, but Amanda was not ordinary. Because of her extreme vulnerability, she felt abandoned by Brook. Dane had been right about that, at least.

Brook had taken some child psychology courses when she had decided to concentrate on illustrating children's books, wanting to understand all that she could about her audience. She knew that the death of Amanda's mother while bringing the child into the world could have given Amanda deep-seated guilt feelings that she wasn't even consciously aware of. Along with a growing understanding of how her mother had died, having a father who was usually too busy to spend time with her could easily have been seen as "proof" of her guilt. Brook was too tender-hearted to risk adding more "evidence" by refusing to see Amanda anymore.

When she left her hotel the next morning after breakfast, she headed directly for the beach. Amanda and Rosa were in the same area where she had always found them before.

Catching sight of Brook approaching, Amanda flung down the small shovel with which she had been digging in the sand and ran to meet her. "Daddy said you might be here today!" she cried as Brook hugged her.

Rosa greeted Brook gravely, as Amanda tugged at her hand. "Come and look at what I'm building. I'm trying to make it look like one of the houses I saw on St. George Street."

Brook sat down on the sand beside the little girl. "Umm," she observed, "that's the Gallegos house."

Amanda beamed. "You can really tell?"

"I'd know it anywhere," Brook assured her.

Amanda surveyed her creation with satisfaction. "Next I'm going to try to build the long porch along the side."

"The loggia?"

"Is that what it's called?" Amanda frowned. "I can make the posts out of sand, but I can't figure out how to keep the roof from falling in."

"You might make it out of cardboard," Brook suggested. "Here." She took a sketch pad from her

71

straw bag and tore off a piece of the cardboard backing, handing it to the child.

"Hey, I think that'll work! Oh, I almost forgot to tell you. At breakfast this morning, Daddy said we could have a picnic. We're going to invite all our friends here and take the Aphrodite to an island that Daddy knows about. He said we could stay all day. Won't that be fun?"

"It sounds great," Brook said, smiling at the child's bubbling eagerness. Amanda was certainly in a good mood today. Was it merely because Brook had come to see her? She wasn't immune to a certain feeling of gratification at the thought, but at the same time it was sad if it were true. It merely showed how lonely Amanda really was.

"We're going on Saturday," Amanda went on happily. "We'll leave at nine o'clock. Can you be at the dock by then?"

Amanda's blithe assumption that Brook would be going on the picnic brought her up short for a moment. Finally, she laughed. "Wait a minute. I can't take a day off for picnicking. Besides, you shouldn't go around inviting people places without asking your father."

"Oh, I already asked him. He said I could invite anyone I like because it's really my picnic. So can you come?"

Brook was already shaking her head. "Oh—I don't think so, honey."

"Please!" pleaded Amanda earnestly. "You could work real hard every day until Saturday, couldn't you? You could even work Sunday if you had to."

Brook sighed helplessly. Sensing her vacillation, Amanda hurried on, "I think Tanya will be there and if you don't come, I know she'll bug me—and try to make friends with me. She always does that."

72

"Why can't you let her be your friend?" Brook inquired, trying to suppress a smile.

"Because she doesn't really want to be friends. She just wants to make Daddy think she does. Didn't I tell you she wants to marry Daddy?" Amanda's small face took on a sorrowful expression. "I know I'll hate it if she ever does!"

"Amanda, I don't think we should be talking about your father's friends like this."

"Okay," agreed the little girl, shrugging. "But you will come to my picnic, won't you?"

Knowing that Amanda would see her refusal as another rejection, Brook finally agreed.

On Saturday morning, Brook dressed in belted khaki bermudas, a white knit shirt with narrow shoulder straps, and straw sandals, tucking a bikini into her straw bag. When she arrived on the dock at nine o'clock, Amanda, wearing a blue swimsuit, was sprawled in a deck chair in the cockpit. She saw Brook immediately and ran to meet her.

Guests were already sunning themselves in various spots about the deck, and Brook heard voices issuing from the salon. Dane was on the upper deck with the young boy Greg, another man, obviously an employee, and an attractive auburn-haired woman wearing a white fishnet jacket over a black bikini. Amanda took Brook into the salon, where six or seven scantily clad guests were being served orange juice, coffee, and Danish pastries by Rosa.

Brook accepted only coffee, since she'd already had breakfast, and was introduced to the other people in the salon by Amanda, who had apparently been instructed to see that all the guests knew each other. In all, there seemed to be about fifteen guests on board.

A few minutes later, Brook was seated on a corner of the long couch, sipping her coffee with Amanda munching a Danish at her feet when one of the guests, whom Amanda had introduced as Alex Revard, came over to sit beside her.

In his mid-twenties, with brown hair and eyes and a deep tan and wearing yellow swimming trunks with an open shirt to match, Alex Revard was a very attractive young man.

"I haven't seen you around before, Miss Adamson. It is Miss, isn't it? Say it is, or my day will be ruined."

Brook laughed at such brazen flirtation, knowing that it was in fun. "It's Miss," she confirmed. "But call me Brook. And you're Alex, aren't you?"

"Right, and also very unattached." He tugged lightly on Amanda's ponytail, causing her to giggle. "I'm waiting for Miss Darcy to grow up."

Amanda twisted her head around and grinned at him. "You're going to get older, too. I think you'll be too old for me, Alex."

He rolled his brown eyes, pretending to be offended. "You really know how to hurt a guy, kid." Then he leaned down and whispered hoarsely, "Can you keep a secret?" Amanda nodded emphatically. "I plan to remain twenty-six all my life."

Amanda looked up at Brook. "He can't do that, can he, Brook?"

"If he can, I want to know how," Brook returned.

Amanda got to her feet. "I'm going to get another Danish."

When she was gone, Alex Revard turned his attention back to Brook. "Have you known the Darcys long?"

"Only a few weeks. I met Amanda on the beach one morning and we became friends. I came today because she told me it was to be a party for her."

She glanced around doubtfully. "It seems an odd assortment of guests for a seven-year-old."

Alex laughed. "You're looking at the idle rich, Brook, an odd assortment under any circumstances. For most of the year we drift from Florida to the Caribbean to the French Riviera. We run into each other everywhere we go and we hang together—maybe because nobody else can put up with us. Some of these people have children tucked away at home with the servants or at boarding schools. Dane had some quaint notion about keeping his daughter with him this summer. You may have discovered that he has quaint notions about a number of things—such as working when he already has more money than he will ever need."

Brook's dark brows rose slightly. "You mean you don't *do* anything?"

He gave a Gallic shrug. "On the contrary. I ski in Sun Valley. I sail. I collect Asian art. I do everything I want to do because I was fortunate enough to have a father who made several million in oil. But I'm not a workaholic, like Dane." He looked at her askance. "No! Don't tell me you're another one."

Brook shook her head, trying to imagine such a life as Alex Revard described. It might be fun for a while, but surely it must become boring, even depressing, in time. "I really don't know. I have to work for a living, so I've never had to decide what I'd do if I didn't need my wages. I can't imagine giving up illustrating altogether, though."

"You're an illustrator?" He seemed extremely interested in the information; perhaps it was the novelty of finding himself in conversation with an honest-to-goodness wage-earner aboard Dane Darcy's yacht. "You're in advertising then?"

"I was for a while. Now I illustrate children's books. That's why I'm in St. Augustine. I'm doing the illustrations for the new Lloyd Pennington book. Are you familiar with his work? He's written a couple of adult novels in addition to his juveniles."

Alex chuckled good-naturedly. "Hardly. I read the book review section of the paper so I can sound intelligent when other people talk about the latest best-seller. People can be snobs about that sort of thing."

Brook smiled hesitantly, wondering if he was teasing her. But, no, she decided, he meant it. She couldn't imagine someone as wealthy as Alex Revard seemed to be feeling a need to pretend about anything. But maybe he enjoyed putting something over on his jet-setting friends.

"It would seem," she said, "that Amanda doesn't know a single child in St. Augustine. She did tell me that she had a friend named Linda in Miami." She finished her coffee and set the cup on the table at her elbow. "I've gotten the feeling that Amanda leads a rather isolated life."

"That's probably true," Alex agreed. "Dane's been very careful about where she goes and with whom, since that kidnap attempt a couple of years ago."

"*Kidnap* attempt?" Brook stared at him. "Somebody tried to kidnap Amanda?"

He nodded. "Two men came into the Darcy backyard in Miami where she was playing. Fortunately a gardener was working nearby. He was on his knees trimming shrubbery, so the kidnappers didn't see him. When he realized what was happening, he let loose with shears, trowels, and shovels— everything he had. One of the men was injured rather seriously when a pair of shears slashed his leg. They got away then, but the police picked them up a few days later."

She could almost see the scene he was describing,

76

could almost feel the uncomprehending fear the five-year-old Amanda must have experienced. And it explained Rosa's extremely protective attitude toward the child. The housekeeper was literally afraid to let Amanda out of her sight unless she was with her father or some other trustworthy adult.

The yacht was moving now, and most of the guests in the salon had wandered out on deck. Amanda returned to ask Brook to go out with her. "We can sit in the sun and play Old Maid." She produced a deck of cards. "You want to play with us, Alex?"

"Sure," Alex agreed, as he followed them out of the salon. "Although, as I recall, you cleaned up on me the last time we played."

Amanda grinned. "You don't pay attention."

Alex slanted a sideways glance at Brook. "I think she's in training to be a professional card shark. She plays pitch like a veteran."

They found an unoccupied spot on deck and spread beach towels from a stack nearby to sit on. Alex took off his shirt. "Didn't you bring a swimsuit?" he asked Brook.

"Yes, but I don't want to get too much sun today. I may need to borrow your shirt if we stay out here long."

He placed the shirt beside her. "Help yourself."

"Daddy said we'd have time to swim before lunch—after we get to the island," Amanda informed them.

"Where is this island?" Brook asked.

"Down the coast several miles," Alex said. "Belongs to a business associate of Dane's. He's in Europe, as I understand it, and offered Dane the use of the island and his villa there while he was gone. It's really a beautiful place."

Sometimes, Brook thought ruefully as Amanda dealt the cards, it's very convenient to have wealthy friends. Most of the other guests were ignoring them, and Brook suspected that they sensed she wasn't one of their kind. She had caught several of them eyeing her curiously, but none of them had made friendly overtures.

As they began to play cards, Dane strolled onto the deck with the auburn-haired woman at his side. She had removed her fishnet cover-up, and the bikini certainly hid none of her voluptuous figure. They approached and Dane said, "Brook, you've probably met everyone but Tanya. Tanya Williams, Brook Adamson." He hesitated momentarily, raking Brook with an amused glance. "Amanda's friend."

Brook got to her feet, not liking the feeling of the two of them looking down on the top of her head. She shook hands with the woman. "I'm happy to meet you, Tanya."

Tanya tucked her arm through Dane's. "You're sweet to spend the day with our little Amanda." She smiled at the child, who ignored her and continued to study the cards in her hand. "She's been lonely in St. Augustine, haven't you, darling?"

Amanda shrugged. "No." Brook knew this to be untrue and realized Amanda would probably have denied whatever Tanya Williams said, just to be contrary.

A man was calling to Dane from across the deck, and Brook was relieved to see the two walk away, Tanya still clinging possessively to Dane.

They played cards for almost an hour, then Brook and Amanda moved to the shady spot under the shadow of the deck house, and Alex brought them all cold drinks. He seemed to have taken upon himself the job of making Brook feel at home, and she was grateful to him for that. Alex stayed close to her and Amanda until they docked at the small island that was their destination.

Brook went down to Amanda's stateroom to change into her bikini before she and Amanda followed the others to the beach, where most of the guests were already playing in the water. As they waded into the ocean, Alex surfaced in front of them and, laughing, sprayed them with a fine mist of water. The three of them were soon squealing and ducking each other like children, much to Amanda's delight.

They cavorted and swam for a while, then stretched out on the sandy beach to dry before going up to the sprawling, yellow stucco villa. Its architecture was Spanish-style, with a ripple of red tiles on the low-pitched roof and wrought-iron balconies on the second floor. The villa sat on higher ground overlooking the beach, surrounded by lush palms and greenery.

Several times while they were on the beach, Brook was aware of Dane's eyes upon them. He and Tanya were sitting with several other guests a few yards away, and it seemed that every time she glanced in their direction she intercepted Dane's narrow-eyed, look. His expression was, at times, displeased, and Brook wondered why. She tried to ignore him, but eventually she gave up and went back to the yacht to change into her bermudas and shirt again.

When she returned to shore, the guests were trailing up the wide, brick steps leading to the villa. Amanda had gone on ahead, and only Alex lingered at the bottom of the steps, waiting for her. Evidently the others weren't going to change out of their swimsuits before eating, and this made Brook feel a little self-conscious about her own attire. Nevertheless, she would have felt worse walking around in her bikini under those penetrating looks from Dane Darcy.

The villa was lovely. It looked to Brook as if it might have been lifted whole from the coast of Spain. The rooms were huge, opening onto a central courtyard where there were a pool and a waterfall, scattered groupings of lawn furniture, and carefully tended shrubbery and flower beds. A stereo system provided soft background music. A lavish seafood buffet was being laid on a table near the pool by a retinue of servants. Some picnic, Brook thought wryly.

After they ate, some of the guests began to dance.

"Come and dance," Alex said. As he led her to the tiled area of the courtyard, the stereo music switched to a disco tune.

"Oh, no!" Brook wailed as Alex began to gyrate around her. "I'm not sure I'm up to this right after eating."

"Come on!" Alex exclaimed. "Loosen up and have some fun."

Laughing, Brook began to move with the music. She liked dancing, actually, and was not a stranger to disco. Alex was an expert at it, she discovered. Without their bodies touching, they danced around each other, laughing, moving together in perfect rhythm as if they had practiced for hours. Alex's eyes were fixed on her flushed face and, suddenly, she saw excitement blaze in them as if a light had been turned on inside him.

For the first time that day, Brook felt completely at ease. Some of the other dancers had stopped and were watching them. A smattering of applause jolted her back to reality, and she became aware that she and Alex had become the center of attention.

She groaned. "I have to stop! You find another partner and I'll sit the next one out."

As she walked away, she noticed Dane Darcy lounging against the courtyard wall in one corner. He had put on a knit tank top with his blue swimming trunks. For once the beautiful Tanya wasn't at his side. After one brief glance in his direction, Brook avoided looking at him again. But from the corner of her eye, she saw him approaching. She had intended to sit down in one of the wrought-iron chairs that were scattered about, but his fingers curled around her wrist.

"Come with me." Before she could protest, he was steering her deftly through one of the wide archways. He directed her along a hall and into a large room. Closing the door behind them, he leaned against it and studied her for a long moment. "The study," he explained. Then he walked to a highly polished cabinet and opened one of the brass-fitted doors. He brought out a decanter and an ice bucket and poured scotch for them both. He handed one of the glasses to Brook.

"No, thank you," she said, not even bothering to be polite. Who did he think he was, bringing her in here without even asking?

"Take it," he told her, pushing the glass into her reluctant hand. "You look as if you could use it." He touched her elbow lightly and steered her toward the red leather couch that occupied one side of the room. A row of floor-to-ceiling windows draped in loosely woven white fabric took up the opposite wall.

Brook relaxed in the corner of the couch and sipped her drink gingerly. Dane Darcy sat down beside her, his arm resting along the back of the couch so that it was almost touching her. She sat straighter and fingered her glass nervously.

Watching her, he downed his drink and set the glass on the leather-topped table in front of the couch. She deposited her nearly untouched drink there too, saying, "I'd better go back. Alex or Amanda may be looking for me." She half stood and found his hands gripping her waist.

"Dane," she said in cool tones, "you're behaving in a way that I find offensive."

He smiled up at her lazily. "I won't say what I think of the way you've been behaving."

The look in his dark eyes made her shiver. "Hadn't you better get back to your guests?"

"You're a guest," he drawled, "and I've been neglecting you."

"I hadn't noticed," she said dryly.

His hands moved slowly up her arms while his glance traveled over her appreciatively, lingering finally on her soft lips. Brook felt as if the air in the room were too thin all at once, and her reaction made her angry. Tossing her hair, she tried to change the subject. "I thought this was supposed to be a party for Amanda."

His glance slid up to her gray eyes. "But it is. I expected you to congratulate me on arranging a day's outing for my poor, neglected daughter."

"This is hardly the type of outing I consider suitable for a seven-year-old child," Brook told him.

He laughed softly. "Amanda is having a ball. You have been very attentive to her all morning—when you could tear yourself away from Alex."

She tried to free herself, but his grip on her arms tightened, although the expression on his face did not change. "Amanda and Alex will be looking for me," she said breathlessly.

"I'm certain *Alex* will," he agreed. "You've been flirting with him all day. Alex has been around, but I'm not sure he's experienced enough to handle a clever female like you. Or are you only sharpening your hook to be used on bigger fish?"

She made a contemptuous sound, her gray eyes blazing. "You, I suppose!"

"Forget Amanda and Alex," he said, his voice suddenly abrupt. Without warning, he pulled her toward him, causing her to tumble onto the couch beside him, almost on his lap. His eyes on her face were a glowing blue with black depths that seemed to go on and on bottomlessly. His fingers cupped themselves around her neck, pressing her toward him. The blond head moved downward, and she stared helplessly at his mouth. It came closer so slowly that Brook began to tremble and, unconsciously, her own lips lifted to shorten the suspense.

When the contact was finally made, there was a rush of confused sensations in Brook. She was incapable of thinking, and her arms went around his neck, her body molding itself to his while he kissed her, his mouth moving on hers with sweetly exquisite seduction, and all her nerves seemed exposed and quivered crazily, as if soft fabric were being pulled across them.

She was lifted and pulled onto his lap, as his hands roamed where they chose. He kissed her throat, the moist warmth of his mouth making her feel dazed. His fingers slipped the narrow strap of her shirt from one shoulder, and when his lips invaded the valley between her breasts she heard herself sighing and realized that her hands were stroking the blond hair at the back of his head. The feelings he was arousing in her were breathtakingly sweet and intoxicating, and when he lifted his head she had to bite back a murmured protest. She looked at him with bemused eyes.

His fingers touched her flushed cheek. "You're a very responsive woman," he whispered, "but I'm sure you've discovered that already. Other men must have made you feel like this. Does Alex?"

She gave him a confused, bewildered look, still half-dazed by his lovemaking. Couldn't he tell that he was the only man who had had such a devastating effect on her? She looked into the hard face and knew she had little defense against him. Already her senses flicked to life whenever he came near her. She had to guard her heart now as she had never guarded it before.

She scrambled off his lap before he knew what was happening. The dark blue eyes surveyed her. "Where are you going?"

"Back to the party," Brook retorted.

He sighed wearily and came to his feet. "What game is this?" he drawled. "I warn you, I don't like cat and mouse. So why don't we be frank with each other. What do you want in exchange for your favors?"

All the heat left her body abruptly and she felt an icy chill go through her. "My favors are not for sale, *Mr*. Darcy!" She walked out, leaving him staring after her.

Chapter Five

Hurrying along the hall back to the courtyard, her lungs drew down air with trembling relief. Disco music continued to pour forth from the stereo system. She found Alex teaching Amanda a disco step at the edge of the twisting and turning dancers.

Seeing Brook, the child called out, "Watch, Brook!" She proceeded to move around Alex in a totally uninhibited rhythm. Suddenly Alex swooped her into the air and set her down, giggling, beside Brook.

"I have to rest for a while!" Alex gasped.

Amanda was breathing heavily as well. "Me too. I'm going to get a cold drink." She ran across the courtyard toward the buffet table.

His breath coming easier now, Alex looked thoughtfully at Brook. "You look pale. Anything wrong?"

Brook shook her head. "The noise is giving me a

headache." Her glance raked the gyrating dancers. They seemed more boisterous than before, and she suspected most of them had had several drinks. Her conviction that this was an unsuitable party for Amanda grew.

"Would you like to get out of here for a few minutes?" Alex inquired. "We could take a walk about the grounds."

"Yes," she said gratefully, and he took her arm to steer her toward the archway leading to the front foyer. Outside the music was only a dull thumping sound in the background. "Ah," Brook breathed. "That's better."

They strolled along a stone-paved walk that led, in meandering fashion, around the villa. "I saw you leaving the courtyard with Dane," Alex remarked after several moments. "You didn't look particularly happy about it."

"Mr. Darcy and I seem to have a personality conflict," she said.

He stopped abruptly and touched her arm to turn her to face him. "Did he make a pass?" She saw that the thought angered him.

"What gave you that idea? He has a date."

The sound he made was filled with ironic contempt. "I've known Dane Darcy for a long time. He may be with Tanya Williams, but that wouldn't stop him from trying to make time with some other woman when Tanya wasn't looking. He did make a pass, didn't he?"

He seemed to ready to make an issue of it. He might even go storming back to confront Dane, although why Alex Revard should feel responsible for her, she didn't know. At any rate, it seemed better to give him no reason for concern. So she said evasively, "He's worried about Amanda and thinks I have some influence over her."

Alex made another disgruntled sound and they continued their walk. At last he said grudgingly, "I guess it isn't easy for a man to raise a daughter alone. Not that the kid isn't better off."

Curious, she looked up at him. "What do you mean?"

"Amanda's mother, from what I've heard, wasn't exactly Super Mom." He shrugged off-handedly. "I shouldn't be passing on gossip, though." He bent to avoid a low-hanging mimosa tree. "Where do you suppose this leads?"

They were standing at a fork in the path, where stepping stones angled off to the west. "Let's find out, shall we?" Brook suggested.

Five minutes later they emerged on the beach, where Brook slipped off her sandals and walked along the wet sand at the water's edge. They strolled for some minutes, talking of inconsequential things, getting to know each other a little better. Brook was relieved that Alex did not again bring up the subject of Dane Darcy. She found the young man an amusing companion, but seemingly without any ambition to do anything constructive with his life. He appeared to be content to follow the idle rich from one luxurious watering hole to another for the rest of his life. This attitude Brook found hard to comprehend, but she liked Alex Revard in spite of it.

Before they got back to the villa, he offered to drive her from the dock to her hotel upon their return to St. Augustine, and she accepted. The party was breaking up when they returned to the courtyard, the guests gathering up discarded shoes and towels in preparation for boarding the yacht. Dane was speaking to one of the servants when they entered, and his head turned as he surveyed Brook and Alex with an inexplicable expression. Amanda had spotted them, too, and came running over to say breathlessly, "I've been looking for you. We're going back to the Aphrodite now."

Brook took her hand, turning her back on Dane's look, and they left the villa. When the yacht was under way again, Alex joined a loud group on the foredeck, leaving Brook and Amanda reclining in two lounges that Amanda had laid claim to as soon as they boarded. The little girl was worn out and was soon asleep. Brook closed her eyes and settled comfortably in the lounge, glad that she didn't have to make conversation.

She napped for a short while, then went down to the galley for a cold drink. Neither Rosa nor any of the male servants was about, but she found a can of cola in the refrigerator and sat down in the small breakfast nook to drink it.

She was about to return to the deck when Dane Darcy appeared in the galley doorway. "So—here you are." He took a cola from the refrigerator and folded his lithe body into the nook across the table from her. His eyes narrowed on her as he flipped off the tab opening of the can and dropped it onto the table.

"Is Amanda looking for me?" She prepared to slide across the leather seat to leave the galley.

"No, she's still asleep. I want to talk to you."

"There isn't much left for us to say to each other, is there?" Brook inquired coolly.

He lifted his cola can and drank slowly, his dark eyes continuing to watch her sardonically. "I've a proposition to discuss with you."

She gave him a cold look. "You needn't go on." Her voice was tight. "My answer is the same as it was at the villa. No."

He smiled crookedly, flashing straight white teeth and making her pulses leap in spite of her anger.

"There is more than one kind of proposition, Brook. You misunderstand . . ."

"Oh, really, Dane!" she flared.

"If you will allow me to finish . . ." His response was impatient.

She subsided, sitting watchfully on the exit end of the leather seat. Her alertness seemed to amuse him. "As I was saying," he went on dryly, "I have a business proposition to put to you. Rose has received word from her family in Mexico that one of her brothers, who has been ill for some time, has taken a turn for the worse. Naturally she feels she has to go down there. I'm driving her to Jacksonville tomorrow morning to connect with a flight to Mexico City."

Brook's reaction was guarded. She thought he was telling her the truth, for Amanda had already mentioned Rosa's ailing brother to her. But what was he leading up to? she wondered.

"This will leave Amanda with no one to care for her for a few days. We're behind schedule at the construction site already, and there are deadlines to meet, contracts to fulfill. I have to spend half-days there at the very least. And a construction site is a dangerous place for a child to be wandering about. I need someone to move on board to supervise Amanda while Rosa's gone."

She was shocked, her eyes opening wide. "Me?"

"It would please Amanda."

"But what about Tanya Williams? Or—is she employed?"

He gave a short laugh. "Tanya never worked a day in her life. And I'm quite sure she'd be willing to take over for Rosa, but frankly I don't think she's the most trustworthy person to leave with a young child. She would probably get so involved in shopping or reading a fashion magazine that she'd forget

89

her responsibilities. For very good reasons, I don't want Amanda wandering off by herself." Brook knew that he was thinking of the kidnap attempt, and she was inclined to agree with him about Tanya. From what she had seen of the woman, Tanya was too self-absorbed to be responsible for a child.

"Besides," Dane went on after a moment, "my daughter doesn't like Tanya, which means that Amanda would give her a hard time. I doubt that I'd have a minute's peace the whole time Rosa's gone."

"There must be someone else you can ask. Maybe there's an employment agency in St. Augustine. You might be able to find someone there."

He was shaking his head. "I don't want a stranger looking after my daughter, either."

"I—I couldn't possibly move in here. I still have work to do on the illustrations."

He leaned forward, his elbows on the table, and said with seeming sincerity, "You would be here as Amanda's companion, nothing more. You could continue your work, take Amanda with you. She likes you, and I think she'd listen to you if you told her to stay close by."

She hesitated. Every instinct she possessed told her to refuse to move aboard the Aphrodite at all costs. But there was Amanda to consider. Knowing of the kidnap attempt, she couldn't help sharing Dane's reluctance to trust the child to Tanya Williams or someone hired from an agency.

He saw her indecision. "Would you try it for a day or two? There's a guest stateroom next to Amanda's. You will be perfectly safe."

She looked across at him, feeling great trepidation. The sun-bronzed face was impassive. She knew that she couldn't say no, yet she was almost certain to regret the decision, whatever happened. Even if

Dane kept his word to allow her to be merely Amanda's companion, she knew that she was too aware of him to be living with him in this confined space, with or without Amanda.

Finally, she said, "All right."

He looked truly relieved. "Thank you. I'll drive you to your hotel when we dock and we'll talk about it at greater length."

"I—I can't. I already accepted a ride from Alex."

He frowned. "I feel I ought to warn you about Alex. He's a ladies' man. You shouldn't make the mistake of taking him too seriously."

She gave him an ironic look. "Your concern is touching, although rather hypocritical."

He stared at her for a moment, then shrugged. "Just so you know what you're doing."

She might have issued a stinging retort, but at that moment Amanda ran into the galley. "Did you ask her yet, Daddy?"

He studied Brook's face for a moment, then turned to his daughter. "She's agreed to move in while Rosa's gone—provided you behave yourself."

"Oh, I will! I promise!" Amanda exclaimed, grinning at Brook.

"I have to go on working," Brook cautioned her. "But you can come with me and maybe you can make some drawings, too."

"I'd like that," Amanda responded. "I like art in school."

"Can you be here at eight in the morning?" Dane asked her.

She nodded, and he slid from the nook. "We should be nearing the harbor. Amanda, why don't you take Brook and show her the stateroom she'll be using."

Amanda was plainly so happy about the arrangement that Brook tried to brush her misgivings aside.

91

But on the drive home, when she told Alex what she was going to do, his doubtful response brought all her fears to the fore again.

"The whole thing sounds fishy to me, Brook," he told her. "Are you sure you know what you're doing?" It was the same thing Dane had asked her about Alex, but she wasn't in any mood to appreciate the humor of that.

"I'm doing it for Amanda, and it will only be for a few days."

He looked at her gravely. "Remember one thing, will you? I'm at the Ponce de Leon if you need a friend."

She thanked him, got out of the car and, filled with troubled thoughts, hurried up the stairs to her room.

When she arrived at the Aphrodite the next morning with a small bag containing a few changes of clothing and her art supplies, Dane, Amanda, and Rosa were waiting for her on the dock.

Dane, in a lightweight khaki suit, and Rosa in a dark dress and hat, a suitcase beside her, were in a hurry to leave for Jacksonville.

"I'll be back a little after noon to change clothes and go on to the construction site," Dane told Amanda, bending to kiss her.

For the first time since she had met her, Rosa smiled warmly at Brook, although she seemed rather distracted even then. "You are so kind to care for Amanda while I'm gone, señorita. I am grateful to you."

Brook took the woman's hand in her own. "We'll be fine. Don't worry about us."

Brook and Amanda waved goodbye to the others, then went on board, where Brook unpacked her bag and arranged the few things she had brought in the built-in closet in her room, the fourth and smallest of

the yacht's four staterooms. Rosa had already prepared pancake batter for their breakfast, so Brook,
with Amanda's help, made the hotcakes and fried
bacon.

After breakfast, they cleaned up the galley and
went out on deck. Brook looked through her
sketches, making a list of other drawings she still
wanted to make. After a sandwich lunch, she suggested they go to San Agustin Antiguo so that she
could add the old schoolhouse and jail to her growing stack of illustrations. They left a note for
Dane saying they'd be back before dark and set off,
Amanda skipping happily beside Brook, carrying
the sketch pad and pencil Brook had given her.

The afternoon went well. Brook made several new
sketches which pleased her, and Amanda stayed
close by, making her own childish drawings. By the
time they got back to the yacht, dusk was falling.
Dane was in the galley making a huge pizza with
everything imaginable on it. Amanda confided to
Brook, as they left their art supplies in Brook's
stateroom, that it was the only thing her father could
cook.

Back in the galley, Dane insisted that they sit
down in the nook and be served by him. He seemed
to be enjoying the reversal of roles, and Brook
watched him moving about the small galley in a pair
of cut-off jeans and faded red shirt, humming to
himself, and realized she was seeing a new side of
Dane Darcy. His blond hair fell carelessly across his
forehead, and the hard muscles in his bare legs
rippled as he moved. He was really quite a sexy-
looking man, she thought and reminded herself
again that she must be on guard while she was
aboard the Aphrodite.

The pizza, oozing with cheese, meat, olives and

93

spices, was scrumptious. There was also a tossed green salad and iced tea. The three of them had little trouble eating everything on the table.

"Mmmm . . . wonderful." Brook finished her last piece of pizza and sat back with a satisfied sigh.

"There's ice cream or sherbet," Dane offered, gazing at her from across the table.

"Heavens, no! I couldn't hold another bite," Brook assured him.

"Neither could I," Amanda confessed. "We had one of those big pralines this afternoon."

"Ah ha!" her father teased. "No wonder you can't hold any more."

Brook and Amanda cleaned up the galley while Dane went into his stateroom to pore over blueprints and contracts. For the first time, Brook wondered where Greg, the deckhand, and the other two male servants she had seen on the yacht the day before ate and slept. She questioned Amanda and learned that the three took turns sleeping on a cot in the cockpit, while the other two went to a nearby motel, where a room was provided for them. Whoever slept on board was given breakfast by Rosa the following morning. The other two ate at the motel. Other meals were provided on board, but Dane had made arrangements for all three to eat in a restaurant until Rosa returned. One of the men was a passable cook, however, and would be doing some of the cooking for the Darcys and Brook while Rosa was gone.

"Daddy said you're awful nice to stay with me, and we can't expect you to cook and clean," Amanda concluded.

Brook smiled at the child. "I *like* being with you. But between you and me, I'm not the world's best housekeeper."

"That's okay," Amanda assured her magnanimously. "You draw real good."

Brook laughed and hugged Amanda. "I saw a stack of books in your stateroom. Do we have time for a story or two before your bedtime?"

After showering and dressing for bed, Amanda was tucked in and Brook sat beside the bed to read from a book of children's stories. The little girl was asleep before Brook had read five pages. Reflecting upon how young and innocent Amanda looked in sleep, Brook laid the book aside, switched off the light, and tiptoed from the room, closing the door behind her.

Dane's stateroom door was closed, and she assumed he was still closeted there. But when she went on deck to look out over the lights of St. Augustine, she found him leaning on the railing, similarly occupied. He saw her before she could retreat below.

"Amanda's all tucked in," she remarked, stopping several feet from him and turning to gaze out over the harbor.

"I heard you reading to her when I left my stateroom. You're very good with children. Do you have younger brothers or sisters?"

"I'm an only child, but I'm finding it's easy to have rapport with kids when there is mutual affection."

He was silent for a moment, but she could feel his gaze upon her and turned toward him uncertainly. There wasn't enough light to make out his expression.

"Is Amanda really the only reason you moved on board?" he inquired in a musing tone.

"Yes," she responded with a feeling of frustration that was becoming familiar whenever she engaged in this conversation with Dane. "She needed someone to look after her, and I didn't like the idea of a stranger doing it any more than you did."

"You must excuse my skepticism," he said. "I can tell it irritates you."

"Is that surprising? Ever since we met, you've been impugning my motives."

He shrugged. "My dear girl, what else could I have done?" He paused, then added calmly, "Of all the children on the beach, you chose Amanda to strike up a conversation with."

"Actually, it was Amanda who spoke first." Brook no longer made any attempt to hide her anger. "If you don't believe me, and I'm sure you don't, you can ask her."

"I believe you. But I can't help it if I still find the sudden friendship between you and my daughter a bit odd."

"I know you do," she told him with wry derision. "I'm a little surprised by it myself. For some reason I seem to be a soft touch where Amanda is concerned. I worry about her."

"She's more self-sufficient than you seem to think." There was a lazy smile in the words. "I've seen to that."

"Because you don't want her to grow up to be some man's responsibility. I believe that's what you told me." The contradictions that she occasionally glimpsed in Dane Darcy perplexed her. "For a male chauvinist," she continued in a sardonic tone, "that's quite a liberated attitude."

He laughed softly. "I'm thinking of the man my daughter will eventually marry as much as of Amanda. A too-dependent woman smothers a man. And when he inevitably begins to resent her, she makes him feel guilty about his resentment."

The certainty in his words caused Brook to believe he was speaking from personal experience. Who had clung to him too tightly and made him feel guilty about trying to break free? His mother? His dead wife?

Yet Tanya Williams, who seemed to be the current woman in his life, was definitely the type of woman he seemed determined not to let his daughter grow up to be. It was another of the contradictions in him that puzzled her. She wondered if he were merely fooling himself. He might think he preferred independent women, but actually mistrust that independence as much as he thought he resented the clinging type. She had gotten the impression that he resented *her* independence, at any rate. It was as though he couldn't accept the idea that she could have a full, satisfying life without a man.

As if he had discerned some of her thoughts, he said suddenly, "Alex Revard would be made to feel defensive by someone like you."

She retorted sharply, "I hadn't noticed that Alex feels at all defensive with me."

"He's a woman chaser," he said curtly, his tone gone impatient and hard all at once.

"I expect you would know more about that kind of man than I," she responded tartly. He had a nerve, criticizing Alex when his own reputation with women was quite notorious.

"Meaning," he drawled, "that I'm in the same category?"

"If one can believe half what is printed in the newspapers, I'd say Alex can't hold a candle to you."

"You surely aren't naive enough to believe newspaper reports," he said dryly.

"Well, I don't have to, do I?" she asked in clipped tones. "The way you've behaved toward me is proof enough."

He laughed. "Is it a sin to try to make love to a

beautiful woman? I can't believe you really think so. Every time I've held you in my arms, you've responded in such an encouraging way."

She stiffened, sensing that he had moved closer to her. She felt heat flare in her cheeks. "I can't stop your imagining things. But at least I can leave you alone with your fantasies. Good night."

She started toward the galley stairs and found him suddenly in front of her. He had moved so quickly and so silently that she was taken by surprise. His hand reached out to cup her face in a caressing gesture, and her senses came clamoring to life, as they always did whenever he touched her. Steeling herself, she clamped down rigidly on her emotions and said in grating tones, "Why do you find it so difficult to fail in an attempted conquest? Is your ego so huge that you can't believe any woman could say no to you?"

"I can believe it if she really means it," he drawled. His fingers traced the outline of her lips, making her tremble helplessly. Her traitorous emotions made her want to hit him for being the cause of that betrayal. He looked down into her eyes and seemed to know exactly what she was thinking. His lips twitched, as if she amused him.

Angrily, she thrust his hand away. "I've no intention of telling you anything but good night." She felt suddenly feverish. Fool, she chided herself. When she moved around him, he did not try to delay her, and she ran down the steps, across the galley, and along the narrow hall to the guest stateroom, where she closed and locked the door behind her. She stood for several minutes in the darkness, waiting for her hammering heart to become quiet and telling herself that surely he would believe now that she wanted nothing to do with him.

* * *

She was already awake early the next morning when Amanda knocked at her stateroom door. Brook allowed the child to come in while she performed her morning toilette and dressed in comfortably worn aqua knit shorts and shirt.

When they entered the galley a while later, the deckhand called Jed, who was a small, wiry, balding man in his fifties, was serving Dane's breakfast.

"Yummy!" exclaimed Amanda. "You made hash browns, Jed."

Jed grinned broadly, exposing a gold tooth in front. "I made them just for you because I remembered that you like them."

Brook joined Amanda on the leather seat facing Dane in the nook. His manner was casual, most of his remarks as they ate directed toward his daughter, and within a few minutes Brook had allowed herself to relax and enjoy her breakfast.

"I'll be over at the construction site all morning," he said as he pushed his plate away and accepted a second cup of coffee. He looked at Brook. "What are your plans for the day?"

"I thought we'd go back to the old town for a couple of hours this morning."

"Have you been to Washington Oaks yet?" Dane inquired.

She shook her head. "I haven't heard of it."

"It's thought to be the first orange plantation in the area, originally owned by an American general whose daughter married a descendant of George Washington. It's now a state park. Quite beautiful. You might get some nice illustrations there. At any rate, you really ought to see it."

"Oh, could we, Brook?" Amanda cried. "We could use the car, couldn't we, Daddy?"

"I haven't been there in some time myself," Dane

replied. "Why don't I drive the two of you there this afternoon?"

Amanda was delighted with the idea. It was clear that the fact that Dane would be accompanying them was as important as the trip itself. The child truly did crave more of her father's attention than she was accustomed to. And since Amanda's presence would insure that Dane would keep his distance, Brook agreed.

Washington Oaks, over three hundred acres of land on Anastasia Island south of Crescent Beach, stretching from the Atlantic to the Intracoastal Waterway, was indeed beautiful. Much of the park had been kept as it must have looked in the early 1800's, when it was part of a Spanish land grant. The grass was kept trimmed, of course, and there were narrow lanes leading throughout the park. But there were trees in profusion, ample evidence of the wilderness it had once been. Brook saw cabbage palms, the buds of which had been eaten by early settlers, magnolias with their dark green leathery leaves and giant flowers exuding a heavy fragrance, pines, and the low spreading live oaks trailing Spanish moss, the trees that marked many Old South plantation sites.

"Didn't you say this was once an orange plantation?" she said to Dane. "I haven't seen any orange trees."

Amanda had run on ahead, having caught sight of one of the many rose gardens that were scattered over the park. Brook had sat down on a bench to make a quick sketch of a giant old live oak tree, and Dane, standing beside her, was watching her deft movements with interest.

"All of the orange trees around here were killed by frost years ago. The plantation owners soon discovered the climate was too uncertain for oranges and sugar and several other experimental crops. Even without the low temperatures, it's doubtful that the soil would have been rich enough for most of the crops they tried. During the early years of St. Augustine's history, the settlers very nearly starved to death, in spite of their efforts at farming. Between supply ships from Spain, they had to depend on fish and what little game they could find."

"The old town has such a romantic air now," Brook mused as she continued sketching. "You forget the people who settled it had some very hard times."

"I'm sure it didn't seem romantic to them," Dane agreed. "It was desolate and dangerous. If they managed to stave off starvation, there were always the hostile Indians and the British to worry about. After the Castillo was built, though, they could take refuge there, provided they had warning of an impending attack."

She finished the sketch and held it at arm's length to study it. "It's good," Dane said. "You're talented. I'd like to see some of your other sketches some time."

She looked up at him. "If you really mean that, I'd like to show them to you. I have some on the yacht."

He sat down beside her on the bench, holding her gaze with his. "I wouldn't have asked if I didn't mean it." She lowered the sketch to her lap. "I shouldn't be surprised," he went on after a moment, "that you're good at what you do. You're so serious about your career." He tilted his head slightly, looking at her through the thick, golden fringe of his lowered lashes.

"Thank you," she murmured, feeling self-conscious about his closeness. His arm was brushing against her own, and she looked out across the park, not wanting to meet his look.

"I've been meaning to tell you," he said. "You can make telephone calls from the yacht, if you want. I'm sure there are people back home you want to keep in contact with."

She glanced at him. "No, only my parents and I've been writing them every week."

The sound he made was somewhere between a grunt and a chuckle. "Surely there are men in Kansas City sitting by their phones waiting for your call—a man, at least."

She shook her head. "I've been dating someone for a couple of years, but we decided to part company before I came to St. Augustine."

"We?" he inquired curiously. "Was it a mutual agreement?"

"More or less." She shrugged, wishing that he would not look at her with that crookedly disbelieving smile. "He wanted to get married, and I didn't. It seemed better all around to call it quits. We both agreed on that."

He gazed out toward the live oak tree that she had sketched, idly watching a fat squirrel scooting up the trunk. "Why didn't you want to marry him?"

"Besides the fact that I didn't love him, Rob and I weren't at all well suited. He wants a wife who will stay at home and content herself with taking care of a house and engaging in nice little hobbies."

He turned back to give her a penetrating look. "What line of work is this Rob in?"

"He works in the advertising agency where I was employed until ten months ago."

His light brows rose. "Did he resent your success in illustrating?"

She smiled faintly. "He said he didn't, but I think that he did. I couldn't really blame him for that. It was a little hard for him to see me reaching my goals while he made no progress toward his own. He does some serious painting but unfortunately has never received the recognition he would like to have."

"He felt threatened by your success in your career," he stated, a scornful edge to the words. "I don't blame you for calling it off. He can't be much of a man."

"You can't understand someone like Rob," she said, "since you are unlikely ever to meet a woman more successful than you are. I doubt that you could ever empathize with someone who is less— ruthless." It was the wrong word to have used, and she tried to amend it. "Determined, I should have said."

He laughed shortly. "No, you were right the first time." There was no hint of apology in the admission. She looked into his eyes and they stared at each other in silence for a long moment. His hard mouth was level, unyielding, the midnight-blue eyes holding a sharp glitter.

He drew a long breath. "What is going on behind those beautiful gray eyes of yours?"

Her face flushed at the sudden depths she saw in his eyes. Quickly she thrust her pad and drawing pencil into her straw bag and got to her feet. She felt suddenly weary, the feelings he aroused too strong for her.

He stood abruptly and clasped her arm. She gasped, whirling about, the thick black cloud of her hair flicking against his face.

"I'm glad you recognize the strain of ruthlessness in me, Brook," he said evenly. "It should tell you something."

Her already flushed face took on a deeper color, her eyes too bright with anger—and fear. "What?" she asked shakily.

His face held mockery now. "I think you know what I mean."

He was laughing at her. The dark amusement in his eyes was maddening, but she did not trust herself to give vent to her anger while being held so close against him. "No," she whispered, "I don't."

"Sooner or later, I always get what I want."

In that moment she knew that the main reason she had been invited to stay on the Aphrodite was not to supervise Amanda. Dane Darcy had tried to break down her defenses on previous occasions. In spite of her resistance, he still half-believed that she had designs on him. Getting her aboard his yacht for several days was a further step in his campaign to force her to admit it.

She made herself meet his look. He was silent, staring at her angry face, then dropped his hand and smiled wryly. "I hear Amanda calling. Shall we go?"

Chapter Six

During the next two days, Brook made herself as unobtrusive as possible whenever she and Dane were both on the yacht. She could not avoid him entirely since they took their meals together with Amanda, but otherwise she kept close to her stateroom or Amanda's when he was around. She knew that he was perfectly well aware of what she was doing, and a few times she had found him observing her with amused eyes.

One morning Brook and Amanda were lingering at the breakfast table after Dane's departure for the construction site, when Tanya Williams appeared unexpectedly on the galley stairs.

."Dane! Amanda!" she called liltingly. "Anybody here?" She was wearing an emerald silk, strapless sundress that set off her tan and rich auburn hair to perfection. It was easy to see why Dane kept her around, Brook thought dryly.

Tanya placed one dainty, spike-heeled shoe in the galley, blinking to become accustomed to the dimmer light after the brilliant sunshine outside.

Her gaze traveled to the nook, widening on Brook's face.

"Hello, Tanya," Brook said quickly. "You've just missed Dane. He's gone over to the construction site."

Tanya took several steps into the galley, obviously trying to adjust to the shock of seeing Brook at the Darcy breakfast table.

"What are *you* doing here?"

"She's staying with me while Rosa's gone to Mexico," Amanda retorted, resentment clear in her tone.

"Dane didn't tell me anything about that." Tanya's full lips pouted momentarily. "I'd have been happy to look after Amanda. I love staying on the Aphrodite."

Before Amanda could speak again, Brook said, "Actually, Amanda and I aren't on board much except to sleep. I'm giving her art lessons." This was true to a degree, since she had been offering a few pointers to help Amanda improve the drawings she made while Brook worked. She hoped that knowing she was instructing Amanda might allay some of Tanya's obvious suspicion.

Amanda slid from the nook. "I'm going to get my sketchpad, Brook. Are we leaving now?"

"In a few minutes," Brook told her. When the child had left the galley, she said, "Would you like a cup of coffee, Tanya?"

Tanya accepted, taking the seat vacated by Amanda. "I wasn't aware that you were such a close acquaintance of the family." The edge of sarcasm in her voice was unmistakable.

"Oh, I'm not. Amanda and I are friends, that's all."

Tanya sipped her coffee, peering at Brook over the rim of her cup. "How long will you be in St. Augustine? Don't you have a job to get back to?"

"I free-lance," Brook explained, "which means that my schedule can be rather flexible. But I'm still working every day and, when I've finished the job, I'll have to return to Kansas City. I have family and friends there. I expect Rosa to be back long before that, though."

Tanya was looking at her speculatively. "Do you have a boyfriend in Kansas City?"

Seeing it as the only way to quell the suspicion that was clearly growing larger in Tanya's mind, Brook said carefully, "I see a lot of one man—Rob McAnnally. He works for the advertising agency where I was formerly employed. We—we have a lot in common."

Tanya seemed to accept this, for her posture on the leather seat became more relaxed. "What kind of illustrations are you doing?"

Glad to talk about the safe topic of her work, Brook told her a little about Lloyd Pennington's book. "Amanda and I are going to the Castillo today so that I can make a few more sketches inside," she concluded. "It played such an important part in St. Augustine's history."

"You've been up to Fort Caroline already, I'm sure," Tanya observed.

Brook shook her head. "Not yet."

"But the history of St. Augustine isn't complete without a trip to Fort Caroline," Tanya responded. "It was established by the French and captured by the man who settled St. Augustine."

Brook smiled. "Menendez. Yes, I know. I want to

go there before I return home, naturally. I thought I'd do it on my last day since I'll have to rent a car for the trip. That way I'll only have to come back as far as Jacksonville for the return flight."

"There's no need for you to be out the expense for car rental," Tanya told her. "I'm sure a single working woman doesn't have money to throw away. I'll be happy to drive you and Amanda up there. In fact, I'd like to. I'm getting awfully bored here with Dane's working all the time."

Playing for time, Brook inquired, "Do you live in St. Augustine?"

"My father has a house here. We usually come for a few months in the spring. Most of the year we live in Miami."

Brook finished her coffee. "I envy you this Florida climate. Kansas City can get really cold during the winter." She set her cup down. "I don't mean to be rude, Tanya, but I must get to work."

"Fine," said Tanya. "I think I'll drive over to the construction site and look in on Dane. I'll pick you and Amanda up at nine tomorrow morning for the drive to Fort Caroline."

Hesitating, Brook said, "I wouldn't feel right about accepting. It's too much of an inconvenience for you."

"Not at all," said Tanya flatly. "I *want* to do it. See you tomorrow."

Brook knew that to protest further would make her aversion to spending time with Tanya too evident, which Tanya would undoubtedly ascribe to a more than friendly interest in Dane on Brook's part. Tanya would think that Brook saw her as a rival, and she didn't want that. "It's thoughtful of you," she said finally. "We'll be ready at nine."

When Brook told Amanda of the plans for the

following day as they walked to the Castillo, the little girl was more free with her opinion of Tanya's motives than Brook had been.

"She just wants to hang around me and try to get me to like her," Amanda exclaimed.

Brook knew that Amanda was right, at least partially, but she treated the subject lightly. "It won't hurt you to be nice to her. A person can't have too many friends."

"I want to go to Fort Caroline," Amanda admitted. "Rosa never takes me anywhere but the beach. But couldn't you and I go without Tanya?"

"That would be too obviously rude," Brook said. "Besides, I've already accepted her invitation. We're going tomorrow, and I'll be very disappointed in you if you aren't polite to Tanya."

"Okay," Amanda grumbled. "I'll do it if I have to."

"Thank you," Brook said, suppressing a smile at the child's scowling countenance. "It'll be good practice for you. You can't go around insulting people just because you don't like them very well." In spite of what she told Amanda, however, Brook dreaded the next day.

The drive up the coast proved to be less of a strain than she had expected, though. Amanda had apparently decided to forget her suspicions about Tanya for the trip and watched for the school of porpoises that had been sighted in the area in recent days, exclaiming hopefully over every unusual ripple on the ocean's surface.

Tanya engaged Brook in a conversation about the coming fall's fashions, a preview of which she had seen in New York in February. She was having an entire new fall wardrobe made by her favorite

designer, she told Brook, and went on to describe
each garment in some detail. Brook tried to appear
interested, murmuring brief responses in the appro-
priate places, for the subject was, at least, a safely
trivial one.

They reached their destination well before noon
and joined a group ready to depart on a tour of the
site. In 1564 the French had sent a group of Huguenots to establish Fort Caroline as a base from which
the French could attack the Spanish West Indies
and the Spanish treasure fleets in the Gulf Stream
near the Florida coast. When the Spanish arrived
the following year at St. Augustine, they marched
north through mucky swampland in the middle of a
torrential rainstorm to destroy the fort built by the
Huguenots. The French who managed to escape
the fort later surrendered to the Spanish and were
either massacred on the spot or sent to Havana as
prisoners.

Now a state park had been established on the site,
and the fort walls had been reconstructed. After a
long walk through the woods to reach the fort,
Tanya sat on a grassy mound of earth and patted her
perspiring face with a tissue while Brook wandered
about, with Amanda at her heels, making sketches.
Once she glanced at Tanya's hot and fretful countenance, as the auburn-haired woman brushed her
hair away from her face and looked supremely
bored. Brook felt a pang of sympathy for the other
woman, but she reminded herself that the trip had,
after all, been Tanya's idea. As long as she was
there, Brook meant to make the most of it so that
she wouldn't have to return.

When Amanda grew tired of drawing, she ex-
plored every nook and cranny of the sod and wood
fort, clambering up the steps to the earthen platform

to look down at the St. John's River. "How many people lived here?" she called down to Brook.

"Several hundred, I think," Brook responded absent-mindedly, concentrating on the cannon she was sketching.

"Gosh, they must have been awful crowded," Amanda said.

Looking up, Brook let her gaze rake the interior walls of the fort. Amanda's remark made her think more deeply about what it must have been like there in 1564. Probably some of the settlers had built rude houses outside the fort walls, but there must have been times when they were all inside. From what she had read, she knew also that most of the Huguenots had been sailors and soldiers, not farmers, and the alien wilderness around them had not provided food in abundance. As well as being cut off from people and land that they knew and living crowded close together for protection and to stave off loneliness, they had often gone hungry. She shivered suddenly, in spite of the humid heat of the day. To tourists the site seemed quaint and interesting, but it must have been dreadfully unpleasant for the Huguenots.

She noticed that Tanya had moved into a spot of shade and, finishing the sketch on which she was working, she took pity on the pampered auburn-haired woman.

Calling to Amanda, she walked to where Tanya sat. "I think I have enough sketches," she said. "I'll buy that book I saw in the museum. It gives a detailed history of the fort with accompanying drawings."

"Can we get a cola before we leave?" Amanda asked.

Brook gave her some coins. "Go on ahead if you want to, but wait for us in the museum."

Amanda ran from the fort to follow some school children being herded about by their teacher. Brook and Tanya followed along the narrow, wooded trail at a slower pace.

"I'm afraid this hasn't been very pleasant for you," Brook said apologetically.

Tanya mopped her forehead with a fresh tissue and glanced sideways at Brook. "I'm fine," she replied a little crossly, and Brook bit back the remark she had been about to make concerning the fact that Tanya looked overheated.

As Amanda and the group of school children rounded a bend in the path ahead, Brook stepped up her pace to keep them in sight. Tanya touched her arm to detain her. "I'd like to talk to you about something before we catch up with Amanda."

Brook glanced at her and slowed her pace. "What?"

"Amanda. It's probably no secret to you that she resents me because of my relationship with her father."

Brook carefully avoided meeting Tanya's sharp blue gaze. "Neither Amanda nor her father has said much to me about it."

Tanya was frowning. "She acted a little more relaxed with me today, don't you think?"

"Amanda has seemed very much at ease," Brook replied, wishing that Tanya would not pursue the subject.

Tanya halted suddenly. "Did you tell her to be nice to me?"

Brook sighed. "Not exactly. I—I just reminded her that a person can't have too many friends." She looked ahead where the path disappeared in the trees. "We'd better go on. I want to catch up with Amanda."

She felt Tanya's curious glance resting on her as they resumed walking. Finally the other woman said, "You do seem to have a way with the child. I suppose that's why Dane asked you to look after her for a few days."

"Yes," Brook murmured.

"You can be a big help to Dane and me."

Brook looked over at her in surprise. "Oh?"

"We want to get married, but we both think we should wait until Amanda can accept me as her new mother. She seems to like you. You could get her to accept me."

Brook wondered how much of Tanya's statement was wishful thinking and how much was truth. A brief image of Dane and Tanya together flicked across her mind, but she brushed it aside quickly. "Tanya, I don't think there would be a problem with Amanda if you would make an effort to get to know her on her own terms—not just as Dane's daughter. Spend some time with her without her father."

"Do you really think that would help?" asked Tanya doubtfully.

"As long as Amanda doesn't think you're trying to use her."

Tanya's expression was suddenly guarded. "What does that mean?"

"A child can tell when someone likes him, and also when someone's only pretending to like him—for whatever reason."

"But I *do* like her." Tanya sounded affronted. "I think she's a sweet little girl. I'm not used to children, that's all."

"Fine," said Brook, retreating from trying to explain to Tanya the crux of her problem with Amanda. It was clearly falling on deaf ears. "Then there shouldn't be any serious problems."

"Dane and I have discussed a Christmas wedding. I think that's a lovely time of the year to get married, don't you?"

"Ummm," Brook murmured.

"What about you and this Rob McAnnally? Are you planning to marry?"

For a moment, Brook was startled, hearing Rob's name from Tanya. But then she remembered that she had led the woman to believe that she and Rob were still seeing each other in an effort to ease her mind about Brook's presence on Dane's yacht. Now she said noncommitally, "Not in the near future."

Tanya pursued the topic. "It must be lonely for you here without him."

"I've been too busy to feel lonely."

"Why don't you have him fly down for a weekend?"

Brook almost groaned her frustration aloud. Why had she mentioned Rob's name to this persistent woman? "Oh, he couldn't get away. He's working on some important accounts at the agency." She searched frantically for something that would take Tanya's thoughts in another direction. She began to walk at a faster clip as the museum came into sight. "Look, there's Amanda waiting for us."

To Brook's vast relief, Tanya did not again bring up Rob's name on the return trip. They stopped in Jacksonville for a very late lunch, arriving back in St. Augustine before dusk.

Dane was not on board, and as soon as Tanya discovered this she took her leave quickly, saying that she would die if she didn't shower and change into fresh clothing.

Later, over a dinner of chicken salad that Brook prepared, Amanda told her father about their trip.

Dane listened attentively, glancing at Brook now and then.

114

"Tanya was very patient with us while we made our sketches," Brook observed for both Dane's and Amanda's benefits.

"I don't think she had a very good time at the fort, though," Amanda put in.

Dane did not respond at all, but merely gave Brook an intensely quizzical look.

Thinking about it later that night in her stateroom, Brook realized that Tanya had been fishing for information about her on that walk from the fort to the museum at Fort Caroline, and she had used the opportunity to tell Brook that she, Tanya, and Dane had a serious relationship. But Brook also felt that she had convinced Tanya that Brook was no threat to that relationship. She would not have been so sure of this had she known what Tanya intended to do when she left the yacht that afternoon. But she didn't find out about that until two days later.

It was early evening, and Dane had returned from a long day at the construction site, showered, changed, and was sitting on deck with Amanda while Jed prepared dinner. Brook was in her stateroom, the door ajar, reading the book on Fort Caroline's history that she had purchased two days previously. She heard a sound and looked up to see Dane in the doorway.

"There's a man on deck asking for you."

She put her book aside, rising. "A man? Oh— Alex?" It had to be Alex Revard since she knew no other man in St. Augustine. But she hadn't really expected to see him again.

She was perplexed to see derision in his look. "Not Alex. I think it's your boyfriend from Kansas City, the one you supposedly parted company with before coming here. He says his name's Mc-Annally."

"*Rob?*" Momentarily, Brook thought he had to be

joking, but his scornful expression told her otherwise. "What in the *world* is Rob McAnnally doing here?"

"Maybe he got lonely." The tone was hard-edged with mockery. He shrugged. "I didn't ask him."

She went through the galley, where Jed was putting dinner on the table and Amanda was washing her hands at the sink. She ran up the galley steps and crossed the cockpit to the lower deck.

Rob McAnnally was pacing restlessly, his stiff back testimony to a grim determination. He whirled about when she spoke his name and came toward her.

"Why have you come here?" Her mind had been churning with possible explanations ever since she left her stateroom. "Is it Mother—or Dad? Is somebody ill?"

"Nobody's ill. Worried sick, maybe." He spoke in blunt, impatient accents. Then he stared at her, shaking his head as if she had changed almost beyond recognition since he had last seen her. "I couldn't believe it until I saw it with my own eyes. You really are living here, aren't you?" He thrust his hands into the pockets of his cord trousers and continued to stare at her as though she were a curiosity of some sort. "What in *hell* has come over you, Brook? Have you lost your mind?"

Censure and amazement were mingled in his voice and manner. Still trying to comprehend why he had appeared suddenly without warning or explanation, Brook frowned. "You appear to be the one who's behaving irrationally. Will you please start at the beginning and tell me what you're doing here?" It was growing dark, and she peered intently into his face, trying to discern the thoughts behind his shadowed features.

He cursed softly. "Trying to save you from yourself. I get the feeling I may be too late, though."

"You're still not making any sense," Brook exclaimed, her impatience growing. "How did you know where to find me?"

"Someone who is worried about you called to tell me what's been going on. She said you're in over your head with Darcy and badly in need of rescuing. I laughed at first—until she told me you'd moved aboard his yacht!"

"She?" Brook had begun to fume, as it began to dawn on her that he believed she and Dane had become intimate. "Was this call anonymous, or did this 'concerned party' give her name?"

"It was Darcy's fiancée, but she didn't give her name."

The thought had entered Brook's mind before he said it. "Tanya? Tanya called you?" Enraged, Brook exclaimed, "I can't believe it! What is that woman trying to pull?"

"What are *you* trying to pull? That's the pertinent question." Even in the shadows she could tell that Rob's jaw was set inflexibly. "In the name of common sense, Brook, don't you know what kind of man Darcy is? What are you doing on his yacht? He's made an utter fool of you."

Tanya had called him. The knowledge stunned her. But hadn't Tanya told him about Amanda and Brook's real reason for being aboard the Aphrodite? Well, if Tanya hadn't, Brook had no intention of trying to pour oil on the waters. She didn't owe Rob McAnnally an explanation about anything! "None of this is any of your business." Her gray eyes blazed into his. "How *dare* you come here like this!"

"When I told your parents where you were, they were grateful that I wanted to come. They've been trying to reach you at the hotel."

"I've been checking with my hotel every morning. There have been no messages from my parents."

"They called this afternoon—twice."

"After *you* told them about Tanya's phone call?"

"They're worried about you, Brook."

"Oh, fine! You and Tanya Williams have made sure of that, haven't you?" She glared up at him, incredulous, trying to maintain enough calm to tell him what she thought of him. "You have nothing to do with me anymore, Rob—nothing. I resent your going to my parents and trying to involve them in this ridiculous tale of Tanya's. I'll never forgive you for that. I don't know what you hoped to accomplish by coming here, but you've wasted the plane fare." She paused to try to get a better grip on her composure, then continued in rigidly controlled tones. "Stay away from me, Rob!" She turned on her heels and started for the cockpit.

"What do you want me to tell your parents?"

She whirled about. "Nothing! I'll tell my parents whatever I want them to know."

"I'm not leaving St. Augustine," he told her with maddening stubbornness. "I have a room at the Monterey. I'm staying until I'm sure you really know what you're letting yourself in for."

She stared at him, frustration almost overwhelming her, but words failed her. As she hurried across the cockpit, Dane stepped out of the shadows. How long had he been there? How much had he heard?

"A lover's quarrel?" he drawled.

She clenched her fists at her sides, wanting to hit his mocking face—wanting to hit *something*. "Don't you start with me, Dane! One unreasonable, insulting man to an evening is enough."

"Why didn't you tell him to get lost?" he went on, as if she hadn't spoken.

118

"I did!" she ground out.

His soft laugh was lightly scoffing. "Plainly not with much conviction. I heard him say he intends to stay on at your hotel."

She threw up her hands. "He's insane!"

"Oh? I thought you had broken off with him." The words were accusing, and Brook fiercely resented his manner.

"I have!" she retorted angrily. She ran a hand through her tumbling black hair. "He'd never have come here if—" She halted abruptly. She'd almost told him what Tanya had done and, even in her present state of emotional upheaval, she wondered about her own motives. Did she want to cause trouble between Tanya and Dane? And what if Tanya denied making the call? Whom would he believe? She heaved a sigh. "Now he's gotten my parents all worked up because they couldn't find me when they phoned the hotel. I'll have to call them in the morning when I've calmed down."

He was studying her intently. "You're leading him on, Brook," he told her flatly. "A woman as intelligent as you are can break off a relationship if she really wants to. No man flies all the way from Kansas City and storms onto another man's yacht wild with jealousy unless he's been given plenty of encouragement. Your mouth may say 'stay away,' but your eyes say 'come closer.' I am in a position to know."

"What!" She could not believe her ears. "Are you suggesting that I've been leading *you* on as well?" She had almost lulled herself into believing that his original attitude toward her had changed. But his taunting smile was answer enough. She caught her trembling bottom lip between her teeth, wondering wildly how she had allowed herself to be put in such an untenable position. She felt angry tears coming and, rushing past him, ran through the galley with Amanda and Jed staring after her, and closeted herself in her stateroom before the dam broke.

She didn't come out for dinner, turning Amanda away with a promise to see her in the morning when she knocked at the stateroom door a while later. Again and again she had played back Dane's accusation in her mind. It was true that he had stirred feelings in her that she'd never experienced before. It was also true that whenever he had tried to make love to her, although she had rebuffed him, she had done so belatedly at times and with decidedly mixed emotions. But she had never been playing games with him, as he seemed to think. She hadn't been playing hard to get with the intention of making him want her even more. She hadn't!

She lay across her bed long after she heard Amanda going to bed across the hall, and tried to lose herself in unconsciousness. But sleep wouldn't come. Eventually, she got up and went into the galley for a cold drink. She saw no one and, not wanting to return to the confines of her stateroom immediately, she ascended the galley steps to sit for a while on deck. She saw Dane sprawled in a deck chair as soon as she stepped on deck, but she didn't turn back. She wanted to say something to him and now was as good a time as any.

He rose to his feet as she approached. She was grateful for the shadows, for he wouldn't be able to see that she had been crying.

"I've been thinking about what you said earlier," she began hesitantly, then continued on a steadier note, "If I've done anything to make you think I welcome your advances, I haven't meant to."

He was silent for a long moment. Although he was very near her, his face was blurred by the darkness.

Then he made a weary sound, and his hand reached for her. The touch of his fingers on her arm made her start as if she'd received an electric shock. She stepped back, turning away from him to lean against the deck railing. He moved to stand behind her, his hands coming to rest on her shoulders.

"Brook—"

"No." She shook her head, the distant harbor lights picking up shiny glints in her dark hair at the movement.

"I shouldn't have said those things to you. It's just that you can make me so angry." His hands moved gently along her shoulders, sending through her a weakness that was becoming harder and harder to conquer. He turned her about to face him and hauled her against him, covering her trembling lips with his. His slow, lingering kiss completely sapped the little will she had left. She simply stayed in the warm curve of his arms and gave herself up to the sweet yearning inside her. His strong fingers worked themselves down her back in a sensuously familiar motion until they reached her hips and he pulled her hard against him, making her fully aware of his throbbing need. The shock of the contact flooded through her, but she couldn't seem to summon the strength to pull away.

When he lifted his head, she felt dazzled, bewildered. "Are you going to stop tormenting me and admit that you want me?" he challenged huskily. "Say it, Brook."

Now that his mouth was no longer doing its tantalizing work, reality was seeping back into her fogged brain. This man was going to marry another woman. He still believed she was a cheap little schemer to be enjoyed for the moment, then tossed aside. She stared up at him. He was breathing raggedly, his breath warm on her forehead. Her fingers spread against his hard chest, and she pushed away from him. "No—"

He jerked her back against him violently. "You don't mean that, and we both know it." The tone was hard and merciless. "Maybe," he went on after a moment, "I've been using the wrong approach with you. Maybe you're the sort of woman who wants to be forced."

His sudden implacability and what he was suggesting made her feel real fear. Her sharp intake of breath sounded incredibly loud in the nighttime silence. Frantic, she struggled free, throwing her hands up in a protective motion that brought her sharp nails in contact with his cheek.

His head jerked back, an explosive curse escaping him. Brook felt as if she were going to faint. Shaking, she gripped the railing, leaning against it for support.

Behind her she heard Dane's breath coming fast and hard. "What do you want, Brook?" he demanded in ruthless accents. "Name it."

She turned about slowly, trying to comprehend what he was saying. "Want? From you?" Her voice broke. "Nothing." She realized that he was shaking —from passion? Or rage? "Nothing," she repeated wearily, "except for you to leave me alone—please."

For a tense moment the silence between them quivered in the warm night air. Then he said, "I'm a rich man, Brook, and I'm prepared to pay for what I want."

"What are you suggesting?"

"I've been thinking of buying a controlling interest in a large publishing company. I'll put you in charge of the art department. You'll have complete control, do the hiring and firing, the works."

She felt as if the blood had drained out of her body. In the midst of a humid warm night, she felt so chilled that she was shaking uncontrollably. There was no longer any doubt about his true opinion of her. She was little more than a high-priced call girl to him.

"I'm not interested." She managed to get the words past cold, stiff lips.

"You're making a mistake," he stated tersely. "I'm a better lover than Rob McAnnally."

Brook closed her eyes. "Oh, Dane," she moaned silently and swallowed down the dryness in her throat that had become acutely painful. She wanted to hurt him, to wound him as deeply as he had been wounding her since the day they met. She lifted her chin and steadied her voice. "I don't think you're in any position to judge that."

The rejoinder angered him, as she had known it would. He gripped her arms and gave her a shake. "Dammit, Brook," he muttered, "tell me what you want." His fingers wound themselves in her hair, forcing her head back. His face was so close to hers now that she could see the blazing eyes.

"You have only one thing that I'm even slightly interested in," she told him. "Amanda. But I don't think even you would give away your daughter."

Dane swore and wrenched his hand from her hair as if it were a supreme effort of will. And then he released her, turning his back on her and thrusting his hands into his pants pockets as though he did not trust them to remain unrestrained. For one brief moment, Brook stared at his shadowy form, her breathing quick and shallow. I've finally convinced him, she thought with vast weariness and a feeling that was one part bitter regret.

She made her way across the cockpit, thinking

123

that she had become a stranger to herself. She didn't understand how she could respond to Dane Darcy with such strong and confusing emotions while at the same time despising him with a desperation that went so deep that it made her feel physically ill.

Chapter Seven

"That man who came to see you last night is back."
Amanda had been waiting on deck for Brook to join
her for their walk to the old Spanish Mission,
Nombre de Dios. Now she stood in Brook's open
stateroom doorway, looking worried. "I hope he
doesn't make you cry again."

Brook stopped in the middle of gathering up her
sketch pads and pencils and turned to the child. She
hadn't really thought that Rob would try to contact
her again after the things she had said to him last
night. What was *wrong* with him? She couldn't
believe he was merely concerned for her welfare.
Was he reacting so unreasonably because she had
wounded his pride by turning him down and then, as
he believed, taken up with a man she'd just met? As
for Amanda, Brook hadn't known anyone had heard
her crying last night. Of course, she couldn't tell the
little girl that her father had been the cause of those
tears, not Rob McAnnally.

She had to make Rob leave her alone, but first she must wipe that frightened little frown off Amanda's face. "How did you know I was crying last night?"

Amanda came into the room and flopped down on the bed. "I heard you. I wasn't asleep yet."

Brook sat down beside her and brushed a stray wisp of brown hair out of Amanda's face in a fond gesture. "You know, Amanda, people cry for a lot of reasons—not just because they're sad or somebody's hurt their feelings."

"You sure didn't sound *happy*," Amanda told her.

Brook smiled. "No, I guess I was tired from all the walking we've been doing. But I'm feeling fine now. So why don't you finish putting my sketchpads and pencils in my bag while I go and talk to the persistent Mr. McAnnally."

"Are you mad at him?"

"I'm annoyed. But I'll get rid of him and then we'll go to the Mission. Okay?"

Thank goodness, Brook thought as she hurried through the galley and up the steps, Rob waited until Dane was gone to come back. At breakfast that morning, the thin scratch made on Dane's cheek by her fingernails had brought back their confrontation of the night before with all of its unpleasantness. He had been coldly aloof, but she didn't know what he might have done if Rob had arrived while he was still on board.

Rob was in the cockpit this time, pacing restlessly back and forth. He wore jeans and a plaid shirt and had the pale look of a tourist newly arrived from the north. He also looked tired, as if he hadn't slept well the previous night. He saw Brook and stopped pacing.

"Well?" she said coldly.

He tried to give her a conciliatory smile, but there was still too much outrage in him for it to be more than a movement of his thin lips. "I want to talk to you."

"I don't want to talk to *you*, Rob. Didn't I make that clear last night?"

He gazed at her sullenly. "I was hoping that after you'd had the night to think about it you might have come to your senses."

"I guess I'm just a hopeless case," she said with heavy sarcasm. "Go home, Rob."

He began to pace again. "I talked to your mother last night after I left here. She wants to know what's going on—what you're doing on Darcy's yacht."

Brook had been determined to remain calm, but his brazen admission that he'd talked to her mother again was too much for her. "Listen to me, Rob!" she fumed. "I want you to stop discussing me with my parents, do you hear?" She looked away from his pinched face, trying to get control of her voice, which had risen shrilly. Then she went on. "I'll call my mother this morning and explain things to her. I never want to see you again, Rob. Go home and paint a masterpiece or something!"

Anger flared in his pale eyes. "You couldn't resist that little dig, could you?" he demanded. "You love throwing your success in my face. My God, you've turned into a hard woman! I suppose we can thank Darcy for that."

"Rob—" She had regretted her remark the second it was out. "I'm sorry. That was unkind, and I didn't mean it. But you have to understand that there is no reason for you or my parents to be worried about me. I'm staying on the Aphrodite to supervise Mr. Darcy's daughter for a few days."

He was staring at her. "He has his lover taking care of his child?" The pale eyes blinked furiously, and then he made an obvious attempt to subdue his rage and reason with her. "Can't you see what an

127

idiot he's making you look? He can hire somebody to take care of his kid. What happened to his wife, anyway?''

"She died," Brook returned shortly.

"Oh. Well, I'm sure it wouldn't have made any difference if she hadn't. Any man who would carry on under the nose of his own child—"

"Shut up, Rob!" She saw that he had made up his mind about her and Dane, and nothing she could say was going to change it. She only hoped she would have better luck with her mother. "Don't come here again. Mr. Darcy is touchy about intruders and you may find yourself in jail."

His mouth dropped open. Finally, he choked out, "You're in love with him! You little fool! He'll use you and besmirch your name in every scandal sheet in the country!"

."Get off this yacht before I call somebody and have you carried off!" Whatever restraints she had been managing to keep on her temper had burst their bounds. She was so shaken by his accusations that she was actually trembling. He hesitated momentarily, glaring into her flushed face, and then he left the yacht.

Brook sank into a deck chair, her face buried in her hands, and tried to get hold of herself before Amanda saw her. It wasn't true! She wasn't in love with Dane. She lifted her head to stare out over the harbor.

How could she love a man who had done nothing but belittle and insult her since the day they met? She wasn't a masochist! She'd always been rather contemptuous of women who got themselves into painful relationships with men and then excused their actions by saying they couldn't help themselves because they were in love. Love wasn't bitterness and torment and irrational behavior. She had always thought that when it happened to her it would be sweet and joyful—a relationship of light with no dark sides.

And yet—and yet . . . Why was she so affected by Dane's every look and touch? Why was he the only man she'd ever known who could arouse in her such a paroxysm of emotions that she felt as if some force deep inside her—a force that had until now lain dormant—had erupted and was rampaging through her blood? No matter how many things she disliked about him, how much he made her resent him, every time he held her in his arms her senses responded wildly, beyond all reason, and against her very considerable strength of will.

She closed her eyes briefly, shutting out the pictur-esque harbor scene. It was a sickness in her, she told herself—animal sexual instinct and lust that she had thought herself too controlled and civilized to feel. But love, no. That was impossible.

"Did that man leave?"

Brook opened her eyes with a start to see Amanda hovering in the doorway at the top of the galley steps, Brook's bulging straw bag clutched in front of her.

"Yes, he's gone." Brook took a deep breath and went to take the bag from Amanda's small arms. "All ready to go? I have to call my mother from that booth near the beach." In spite of Dane's offer of the yacht's communications system, she didn't want to use it for long-distance calls. "It'll just take a minute, and then we'll walk to the Mission. I'm looking forward to that, aren't you?"

Amanda nodded, her blue eyes searching Brook's face. What she saw there seemed to reassure her, for she smiled.

"After that, how would you like to have lunch in the old town?"

"They had sandwiches in the ice cream parlor."

Brook felt the tension leaving her, and she took Amanda's hand. "Not to mention the best chocolate ice cream in the world. Right?"

"Yes," the little girl agreed and then, as they left the yacht, she began chattering excitedly about the possibility of their catching sight of the elusive porpoises on their walk to the Mission.

Brook's mother proved more reasonable than Rob had been. Brook explained to her how she had met Amanda and how she'd come to move onto the Darcy yacht in Rosa's absence. "That's all there is to it, Mother," she finished finally. "There is nothing going on between Dane Darcy and me, so will you please stop worrying?"

"But Rob seems to think . . ."

"I don't care what Rob thinks! And another thing, Mother. If you and Dad want to continue your friendship with Rob, that's your business. But I'd appreciate it if you wouldn't discuss me with him any more. I've discovered that not only do I not love Rob, I heartily dislike him. He's smug and—"

"All right, all right, dear," her mother interrupted. "I can see it wasn't a good idea for Rob to come down there. Your father and I—well, Rob seemed so upset that we thought there might be something to what he said. We don't want you to get hurt. But I guess we should have tried to stop Rob." She sounded considerably subdued.

"Yes, you should have. But I think he's gotten the message now. I'll call you again in a few days."

When she had hung up, she called her hotel to see if there had been any further word from Lloyd Pennington. There were no messages.

In spite of its strained beginning, the day proved to be a productive and enjoyable one, and she and

Amanda didn't get back to the yacht until dinner-time. During the meal Dane talked little, as did Brook. Afterward Amanda showed her father the drawings she had made that day, and then Brook sent her in to bathe and get ready for bed.

Jed, after cooking dinner, had left the yacht to have his own meal with the other two men employed on the yacht. He would be back later to sleep on the cot in the cockpit.

Brook busied herself cleaning up the galley, ignoring Dane, who finished his coffee in brooding silence. Finally, he carried his cup to the sink. He started to leave the galley, then hesitated and turned back to say, "Brook—"

She turned from the sink, wiped her hands on a towel, folded her arms in front of her, and looked at him with a guarded expression.

"I may have been a little overbearing last night."

"A little!"

A muscle worked at one side of his mouth. "I'm trying to apologize, if any apology is needed."

"If it's needed! You really can't bear to say you've been wrong, can you?"

He thrust his hands into his jeans pockets and looked at the ceiling for a moment, as if he were trying to keep his temper in check. His gaze returned searchingly to her face. "I admit—I may have misjudged you in some ways."

"Oh? In what ways do you think you *may* have misjudged me?" she asked frostily.

His look grew more probing. "I've come to realize that you really are dedicated to your career, for one thing. It's not just a stop-gap measure until you get married." There was a curious, musing quality in his tone now. "I've also seen that you care very deeply about Amanda. I've never known a woman like you,

131

someone who has other interests in life than trying to make some man responsible for her." He looked away, staring at his own wavy reflection in the stainless steel refrigerator door. There was such a dull, lifeless sound to the words that Brook let her guard down a little.

"This isn't the first time you've said something to me about overly dependent women," she said quietly. "Who made you feel this way, Dane? Was it Amanda's mother?"

He turned his head quickly to stare into her eyes. Then he said, "Come up on deck. I don't want Amanda to hear us." When she hesitated he repeated, "Come up on deck, Brook."

She followed several steps behind him until they'd reached the lower deck. "Sit down." He indicated a canvas chair, and when she was seated he stood facing her, legs apart. She was shocked by the pain in his eyes.

"Rebecca, Amanda's mother, was one of the most beautiful women I ever knew. She was from an old, aristocratic southern family. No one had ever said no to her in her life. Whenever she did irresponsible things, which she frequently did, her father always came to the rescue. She was never made to suffer any unpleasant consequences, no matter what she'd done." He took a deep, uneven breath and the narrowed eyes slid away from her for a moment.

"You needn't go on, Dane."

"No." The word was sharp. "You asked a question, and I'm going to answer it." Yet he seemed to be having trouble finding the right words. After staring down at his shoes for a moment, he looked at her again. "Oh, I knew Rebecca was spoiled, but I was young and so was she and I thought she would outgrow the faults I saw in her." He heaved another sigh before continuing. "Our problems started as soon as we were married. I was involved in some condominium projects at the time, in Hawaii and other places. I had a million details and problems to see to, but Rebecca wanted me at her beck and call. She wanted to go jetting off here or there to be with her friends, and she wanted me with her.

"I tried to appease her for a time, but it only made her worse. I couldn't stand the kind of life she wanted to live, and finally I told her so. It got so that every time I returned home—even after only a day in the office—she accused me of seeing other women. She would become hysterical and have to be sedated. And it didn't matter whether we were alone or in public. She threw tantrums and made scenes in some of the best places in Miami."

Brook had been listening with growing compassion. She sensed that he had had this bottled up in him for years. "Oh, Dane, I'm sorry!"

The sound he made was eloquent with despair. "Then she got pregnant. She didn't want the baby. She threatened to have an abortion. Every time I came home she became so emotional that I really feared for her sanity and for the baby's well-being. It seemed that she was worse when I was around, and one night I finally couldn't take any more. I told her I was going to move out of the house." He ran both hands through his hair, and Brook saw that his fingers shook. Then he moved his head back and forth as if to dispel the dark memories. "I was so angry and frustrated that I hardly knew what I was saying. I slammed out of the house, drove to a bar, and got very drunk. I didn't come home until the next day." His sharp intake of breath sounded loud in the heavy silence. "That's when I learned that Rebecca had gone into labor the night before. It was

133

six weeks too soon. I rushed to the hospital, but I was too late. She was dead. And it was touch and go with Amanda for several days."

He turned away from her and gripped the deck railing. There was a long, pained silence before Brook said, "You've been blaming yourself for your wife's death all these years." He did not respond. "Dane," she went on finally, "it wasn't your fault."

"The doctor said Rebecca's anxious state during the pregnancy had contributed to the premature birth and Rebecca's death," he uttered in a muffled voice. "He left little doubt in my mind that he felt I could have helped the situation if I'd been more supportive of my wife."

"I'm sure you tried to be."

He turned to face her, an abject scowl lining his features. "Are you? Well, I'm not so sure. I tried to talk to her, to console her for a while, but then I gave up. I was young and impatient."

"From what you have said," Brook observed quietly, "your wife had made up her mind not to be consoled no matter what you did."

He shrugged ruefully. "I could have given up my work, but I refused."

"Wouldn't that have made you as miserable as Rebecca? How would that have helped her?" Brook leaned forward in her chair, speaking earnestly. "I know it must have been horrible, losing Rebecca the way you did, but you're much too hard on yourself."

After a while, he said slowly, "I don't think you have any idea what a man pushed to the wall is capable of."

She released a long breath. "Maybe not. But I know that you can't force another person to be what he is not, any more than you can force yourself to be someone else. You might fool yourself into believing that you've succeeded for a while, but in a crisis we all revert to our true selves."

There was a pause during which he seemed to be contemplating what she had said. Finally, "I'm convinced of one thing. My true self"—there was a touch of irony in his use of her words—"was changed by my experience with my wife. I decided if that were love, I wanted no part of it ever again."

"You allowed one experience to embitter you," she amended, wondering why she felt angry with him for the confession.

He grunted impatiently. "From what I've seen in the lives of others, as well as my own, love brings more pain than it's worth."

"That's a depressing outlook."

"You'll come to agree with me in time," he said flatly. "Apparently you've never been in love."

"You're wrong. When I was in art school I fell in love with one of my instructors." She was surprised to hear the words issue from her own mouth. She'd never told anyone about that most secret corner of her past before.

"What happened?" There was real interest in the question.

"Oh, we had some pleasant times—until I discovered he was married and had two children." She made a sound of self-disparagement. "I should have suspected from the beginning. He always took me to out-of-the-way restaurants and could never see me on weekends. I was incredibly naive. I—I felt betrayed when I found out."

"You see?" he said quietly. "Pain comes with love as surely as night follows day."

"It did make me wary," she admitted, "but Dane, you can't have the good things in life without risking getting hurt."

He laughed shortly. "You sound very convincing, but you're still shy of men. Anyway, thanks for listening to me—and it hasn't been a total loss. I've at last discovered something we have in common. We've both sworn off love."

She gazed up at him for a long moment. The distant harbor lights illuminated his angled features, but there were dark shadows, too. The expression in his deep-set eyes was lost to her. "I'd better go check on Amanda. I promised to read to her before she goes to bed."

As she started across the deck, Dane spoke her name. When she turned back questioningly he said, "Thank you for taking such good care of my daughter."

She thought about that conversation on deck long after she had retired for the night. What Dane had told her explained some things in him that she had resented—the unfeeling way he seemed to use women, as if he were somehow trying to punish them and at the same time exorcise the disillusionment of his marriage—the way he neglected Amanda on occasion, as if he believed that it could make her more self-sufficient. The revelations Dane had made convinced Brook of something else as well. He would not marry Tanya Williams, or any woman. Whatever Tanya believed—and perhaps Dane was to blame for leading her on—Brook did not think he would ever marry again. His only experience of the institution had been too devastatingly painful from start to finish. She suspected that, at some level, Tanya knew this too, and felt insecure in her relationship with him. It was this insecurity that had prompted her to phone Rob McAnnally and ask him to come to St. Augustine "to rescue Brook." If Dane ever found out what Tanya had done, he would probably be outraged at the woman's proprietary attitude where he was concerned.

Eventually Brook slept, but lightly, her slumber disturbed by dream fragments that seemed to have no meaning or connection with each other. She was glad when she awoke for the fourth or fifth time and found sunlight pouring in through the high windows of her stateroom. She looked at her wristwatch and discovered it was past nine o'clock.

She showered, attended to her hair and face, then dressed quickly in the cotton jumpsuit she'd been wearing on her first encounter with Dane. As she left her stateroom, she heard voices from the galley and realized that Dane and Amanda were already at breakfast. She entered, finding Jed placing golden waffles on a platter, and said apologetically, "I seem to have overslept. Why didn't someone wake me?"

"Daddy said you needed to rest," Amanda told her. Brook glanced at Dane but could read nothing in his face. She sat down beside Amanda in the nook, and Jed served the waffles.

After adding butter and maple syrup and taking a sample bite, Brook said, "Jed, these are delicious."

The little man grinned appreciatively. "Thanks, Miss Adamson, but they can't hold a candle to Rosa's waffles. To tell you the truth, I'm glad she's coming back today to take over the cooking."

Brook looked quickly at Dane. "Rosa called a little while ago," he explained. "I'm meeting her plane in Jacksonville at one."

"Is her brother better?" Brook inquired.

He nodded. "He's had a stroke, but they don't think he will be too severely paralyzed. They've moved him to a nursing home. I checked into the place and it's the best in Mexico. He'll be well cared for."

Brook was certain that such a home must be terribly expensive; she suspected that Dane was footing the bills.

"Do you have to move back to your hotel now?" Amanda asked. An unhappy scowl was turning her mouth down at the corners.

"I'll have to move later on today," Brook told her, "after Rosa returns. But we can still meet on the beach—until I have to go back to Kansas City."

Amanda's narrow shoulders slumped. "When will that be?"

"A couple of weeks," Brook said. "But I'll write to you, and you can write back and tell me what you're doing."

"I won't be doing anything but going to the beach," said Amanda with a sullen little pout.

"When you get back home, you'll be doing lots of things with your friends," Brook told her.

Dane had listened to this exchange without comment. Now he finished his breakfast and said abruptly, "I'm leaving for Jacksonville now. Rosa and I will be back before dark."

Brook and Amanda spent the day on the yacht. They played cards and sunned on deck, and Brook made hamburgers for their lunch. In the afternoon, she packed her belongings to be ready for her departure as soon as Rosa and Dane arrived.

To her dismay, she felt reluctant to leave. It seemed to her that she had been living aboard the Aphrodite for much longer than a few days, and leaving was going to be sadder than she had anticipated. Foolishly she had allowed herself to become too emotionally involved with Amanda. She would not let herself speculate about how emotionally involved she was with Amanda's father.

After Dane and Rosa's return, Dane gave Jed the keys to the Cadillac and instructed him to drive

Brook to her hotel. She was relieved that Dane had not insisted on driving her himself. She did not want a leave-taking without the protective presence of Amanda and Rosa. She assured the Mexican woman that everything had run smoothly in her absence, hugged and kissed Amanda and promised to meet her on the beach the following morning, glanced briefly into Dane's inscrutable face to say good-bye, and followed Jed from the yacht.

Back in her hotel room, she immediately called the desk to see if Rob had checked out and, to her relief, was told that he had. She unpacked and took a long, relaxing bath, telling herself that it would be pleasant not to have to worry about anyone but herself for the remainder of her stay in St. Augustine. Somehow she did not feel as happy about the prospect as she should have. After dressing she had dinner in a restaurant near the Monterey, returning to her room about nine.

But she couldn't get interested in reading a book or looking through her sketches, and she ended up pacing restlessly about her room, feeling ridiculously bereft.

Finally she ordered a pot of coffee from room service and took it out to the balcony where she lingered for a long time, gazing out across the bay to the lights of Anastasia Island. Tomorrow, she told herself, she would get back to work with a vengeance. Caring for Amanda had cut into her working time. Yet she couldn't help feeling a pang of regret that she wouldn't be spending much time with the child now. And she probably wouldn't see Dane again.

This last thought had slipped into her reflection unaware. Immediately she assured herself that with hard work she would have practically forgotten the Darcys by the time she returned to Kansas City.

Certainly she must forget Dane and the unfathomable hold he seemed to have on her senses. She wondered unhappily if she were in love with him, as Rob had said. But then she told herself that she couldn't allow herself to be. Dane Darcy wanted nothing of love; he had told her so.

Chapter Eight

"Can't you stay a little longer?" Amanda's blue eyes were fixed mournfully on Brook's face. Remembering Dane's observation that bright children were better at manipulating adults, Brook tended to agree with him. It was the third day since she had left the yacht, and on each of the previous two mornings Amanda had tried various approaches to get her to prolong their time together on the beach. Today's tack, it appeared, was to be a bid for sympathy. The child sighed loudly. "Daddy's been leaving the Aphrodite before I wake up and getting back after I've gone to bed." Amanda pushed over a partially constructed sand castle with her bare foot. "I'm getting tired of playing in the sand, too."

Rosa, who was sitting on the nearest bench within hearing distance, said, "Your father explained to you, child, that he has construction deadlines to meet."

Amanda frowned fretfully. "I don't care. I wish I'd stayed in Miami."

"Well, I don't," Brook said cheerfully. "I'd never have had the privilege of meeting you if you had." She got to her feet, brushing sand from the back of her shorts as she did so.

Amanda looked up at her. "Tanya hasn't come to the Aphrodite since you left. Do you think Daddy told her to stay away?"

Brook felt her heart skip a beat, then increase its rhythm. Was it possible that Dane had severed his relationship with Tanya? But immediately she felt perturbed with herself for the small flare of hope Amanda's words had aroused in her. What difference could it make to her if Dane and Tanya were no longer seeing each other? There would be another Tanya in Dane's life soon enough. There were always several candidates waiting in the wings, she was sure.

"I have no idea what your father has told Tanya," she informed Amanda. She hitched the strap of her straw bag over her shoulder. "I really have to go now. Maybe I'll see you tomorrow."

"Please—" Amanda began in wheedling accents.

"No," Brook said firmly. "I've already stayed nearly an hour." She bent to brush straggling strands of brown hair away from the child's eyes. "See you later. Okay?" She said goodbye to Rosa, then walked briskly away. She couldn't help feeling sympathy for the child, but she couldn't let herself get more involved with Amanda. She was Dane's and Rosa's responsibility, and Brook's St. Augustine assignment was responsibility enough for her.

Since leaving the Aphrodite, she had been so busy during the days she actually had little time to think about Amanda or anything else but her work. The

142

evenings, on the other hand, seemed to drag out much longer than they had when she first arrived in St. Augustine. Therefore, when Alex Revard called her at six that evening and asked her to have dinner with him, she was happy to agree.

She'd purchased a tiered, lace-trimmed skirt and hand-embroidered peasant blouse that day in one of the old town's little shops, and dinner with Alex gave her an occasion to wear them. She pulled her thick hair atop her head and fastened it with combs, arranging the ends in a cascade of loose curls.

When Alex arrived at eight, wearing linen trousers and a green shirt, he commented, "You're ravishing! Did you make yourself so beautiful just for me?"

Brook laughed at the teasing twinkle in his brown eyes. "Actually, I just bought this outfit today and your dinner invitation gives me a chance to show it off."

"So I'm only an incidental convenience?" he inquired with pretended disappointment. "Oh well, I'll settle for that."

As they left the hotel in Alex's Ferrari, he asked, "Do you like Italian food? Cumbadi's over on the island is excellent."

"Sounds wonderful," Brook agreed.

The restaurant was on Anastasia Boulevard, across the Bridge of Lions, and proved to be all that Alex had led her to believe. He ordered for both of them: baked clams oreganata as an appetizer and a main course consisting of a variety of rich Italian dishes—manicotti, lasagna, stuffed shells, ravioli, ziti and sausage—along with an excellent imported wine.

After her salad and appetizer, Brook sampled a bit of each food in the main course, but she couldn't begin to eat everything on her plate. "This is delicious," she groaned finally, laying her fork down and sitting back in her chair, "but I'm afraid my stomach has reached its capacity."

Alex, who seemed to have an enormous appetite for such a slender person, returned, "Just sit there and sip your wine then and watch me do justice to my meal."

"It's a pleasure to watch someone who enjoys eating so much," Brook told him with a laugh. "The chef will love you."

Alex suddenly looked past her toward the door of the restaurant. Then he smiled and waved to someone behind her. She looked over her shoulder to see Dane and Tanya Williams following the hostess to a table. Dane saw them and, after a narrowing of his eyes that suggested surprise and disapproval, he nodded. Brook looked away quickly, picking up her wine glass and discovering, to her irritation, that her hand shook slightly.

Alex regarded her curiously. "You look—uncomfortable. Does it bother you that Dane and Tanya are here?"

She set her wine glass down. "Of course not. Why should it?"

His head tilted slightly to one side, he continued to study her with interest. "I don't know. Did something unpleasant happen while you were living on Dane's yacht?"

"No," she told him. She glanced aside briefly from the corner of her eye and wished that Dane and Tanya hadn't been seated at a table directly across the room from theirs. She would have to see them if she turned her head even slightly.

"We can go if you want."

She looked at Alex's plate. "Don't be silly. You haven't finished your dinner." She smiled at him.

144

"Besides, you're imagining things. I don't mind at all sharing a restaurant with Dane and Tanya. In a town this size, it's impossible to avoid anyone for very long—not that I want to avoid them. It doesn't matter to me, one way or another."

"Good," Alex said, attacking his meal again.

Brook sipped her wine slowly, aware of a prickling at the base of her skull, a sensation of being watched. She knew that if she should turn her head she would see Dane staring at her. At least, she told herself grimly, she now knew that he was still seeing Tanya. Not that it mattered to her, but she wished he wouldn't keep staring at her like that. She was finding it more and more difficult not to glance at him. Eventually, she did lose the battle with herself and met his look briefly. His expression remained unchanged, hard and brooding—as if he would like to stare a hole through her, Brook thought with irritation.

She was vastly relieved when Alex finally finished his meal and they could leave. Alex took a long, leisurely drive along the main highway traversing Anastasia Island before returning her to her hotel. In spite of Dane's warnings about Alex, he was an amusing companion, easy to talk to, and his behavior could not have been more proper.

Later, outside her hotel room, he asked her to have dinner with him again the following evening, saying he wanted to take her to a new seafood restaurant. She accepted the invitation without a qualm and said good night.

Once she was alone in her room, the relaxed feeling she'd had with Alex quickly left her. Dane's grim, almost accusing face rose up in front of her and she felt angry with him all over again. The sooner she put some distance between herself and Dane

Darcy, the better for all concerned. She thought she could finish her work in St. Augustine in three or four days and vowed to leave on the coming Saturday.

Consequently, on her second date with Alex she turned down his invitation for a third, explaining that she would have to put in all the time she could manage for the next few days in order to finish the assignment on schedule.

Friday morning when she met Amanda on the beach, she told her she would be leaving St. Augustine the next day. As she had expected, Amanda was not at all happy at the prospect, and Brook spent more than an hour with her, trying to make her understand why she couldn't extend her stay.

"There are other jobs waiting for me, honey," Brook said finally.

"Why can't you just let them wait? If you're running out of money, you can move back on the Aphrodite."

Brook exchanged a glance with Rosa, whose ironic look told Brook that Dane Darcy's daughter could hardly be expected to understand what it meant to be in financial straits. "You know I can't do that, Amanda," Brook said firmly. "I like my work and I want to keep on doing it, but if I'm not dependable publishers will stop giving me assignments." She took a note pad from her bag and printed her name and address on a piece of paper, handing it to the child. "Here's my address. I'll be looking forward to getting letters from you."

Amanda gazed at her doubtfully. "Will you answer them?"

"Certainly I will," Brook assured her. "Now I have a lot to do today, so I must be going." She bent and kissed the little girl's forehead, then straightened quickly to say goodbye to Rosa.

Brook hurried away, swallowing down the lump that had lodged in her throat. Common sense to the contrary, she had allowed herself to love Amanda Darcy too well. She blinked rapidly and tossed her heavy hair back from her face as she stepped up her pace to cross the boulevard. The saddest thing about the situation, she told herself, was that Amanda would probably miss her even more than Brook would miss Amanda, simply because the child would have so much unoccupied time in which to think about it.

In the afternoon Brook walked several miles about the town, stopping now and then to sketch something she'd missed before. Being totally absorbed in her work, she had little time to indulge in self-pity. It was near dark when she finally made her way back to her hotel, the fresh sketchpad she'd started out with that morning nearly filled with new drawings.

With an effort, she dragged her weary body into the shower, where warm water and soap revived her slightly but not enough for her to consider going out for dinner. Instead, she ordered a seafood salad and coffee from room service.

About ten her phone rang; it was Lloyd Pennington. "I've been trying to reach you all day," he told her.

"I've been working," she replied. "It's my last day and I didn't want to miss anything."

"Your last day? You don't mean you're leaving tonight."

"Tomorrow," Brook said.

"I hate to ask this, Brook," Lloyd said, "but can you cancel your plans and stay on a few more days? I'm on my way down. I'm in the Miami airport right now for a short layover. I should be there later tonight."

"Oh, Lloyd, I wish I'd known. My flight's con-firmed and—"

"Are you scheduled to begin another assignment immediately?"

"Not for a couple of weeks," Brook admitted.

"Well, can't you give me three or four days? I really want to go over the sketches with you on the scene, in case I see something you've missed. It's possible. You haven't read the entire text of my book."

Brook sighed, knowing that she would have to agree. She really had no good excuse for insisting on leaving the next day, except that she wanted to be anywhere but St. Augustine as quickly as possible.

"I—I suppose I can stay."

"Good." Lloyd's voice was deep with satisfaction. "Thanks, Brook. I booked a room in the Monterey. How about meeting me in the coffee shop at eight in the morning for breakfast?"

"Fine," Brook said. "I'll see you then." Disconso-lately, she hung up, then called the airlines to cancel her flight for the next day.

Lloyd Pennington was already seated at a table in the coffee shop reading the newspaper the next morning when she appeared for breakfast. The author, in his mid-forties with a shaggy graying beard and a pipe clamped between his teeth, was almost a caricature of an absent-minded professor. Having become very well acquainted with him on the previous occasion when they had worked togeth-er, Brook knew, however, that although he was a professor he was anything but absent-minded.

His pleasant face broke into a broad grin when he saw her, and he got to his feet to give her a bear hug before she took the chair across from him.

"Weren't you able to talk Kim into coming with you?" Brook asked.

148

He shook his head. "She promised me she'd come next time I have to take a trip. I know how that goes, though. One of the kids will come down with the chicken pox or break an arm or something just before we're scheduled to leave. Ah, the trials of a family man."

Brook laughed. "You love every minute of it."

"Yeah," he agreed good-naturedly. "I do. Only, sometimes I try to remember what it was like before we had the patter of so many little feet. Know what? I can't. I don't know how I became a writer. I used to think writers were broody loners, always staring off into space and sunk in thoughts of their next masterpiece. Around my house, that's impossible."

"Masterpiece, eh?" Brook said. "That's one of the things I like about you, Lloyd. You don't suffer from a poor self-image."

"Heck no," he quipped. "No point in denying I'm a genius when all the world knows otherwise."

Brook shook her head in amusement and opened her menu. "All the walking I've been doing has given me a hearty appetite. I hope you're buying, Lloyd."

He leaned across the table and confided, "The publisher is, so shoot the works."

After they'd given their orders to a waitress, Lloyd sat back in his chair and, gesturing with his pipe, launched into a discussion of his manuscript, a copy of which he'd brought along for Brook to read.

Within a few minutes, Brook's reluctance to extend her stay in St. Augustine had disappeared. Lloyd's enthusiasm for the old town's history was contagious, and she was eager to get his reaction to the sketches she had done. They finished breakfast and ordered a fresh pot of coffee to take up to Brook's room, where they would be working.

Once there, Brook poured the coffee and curled

up on the couch to drink hers while Lloyd studied her sketches. Occasionally he would murmur a comment. "I like this one," or "Uh-huh, yes—this is good."

Eventually, he'd seen them all and Brook said, "Now, let me show you the colored drawings I've done as ideas for the cover."

After spreading the drawings out on the carpet and looking them over carefully, he said, "No contest, as far as I'm concerned. It has to be the pelicans with the Castillo in the background."

Brook smiled. "That's my favorite, too."

He picked up his coffee and sprawled in a chair. "The work is up to your usual excellence. There are a few scenes that should be added, though. You'll see what I mean when you read the manuscript. Why don't you spend the day doing that while I scout out the locations I want. That way we can go to the new sites tomorrow without wasting any time. I think three more days ought to wrap things up."

Brook agreed, and they made plans to meet for dinner in the hotel dining room. Over dinner, Lloyd outlined their itinerary for the next day. It sounded rather grueling to Brook, but she made no protest, for the more they could accomplish tomorrow the sooner she could leave. Eventually, Lloyd left off talking about his book and began to regale her with amusing anecdotes concerning his children. She laughed so much that her stomach hurt.

Glancing idly about the dining room, she watched the other diners, who were mostly tourists. There seemed to be an attitude of light-hearted well-being in the room, and it felt good to be a part of it.

Suddenly she felt a prickling of her scalp, and a pall seemed to settle on her mood. She swung her head around, abruptly tense, and felt the color leaving her face as Dane Darcy stared at her over the top of a row of ferns at the far side of the room. Across tables of chattering people, their eyes met.

"Oh no!" Brook breathed.

"What's wrong?" Lloyd turned to follow the direction of her gaze. "What are you looking at?"

"A man I know."

He saw the wince she gave and frowned. "That scowling fellow over there? Who is he? What's he done to make you look like that?"

"His name's Dane Darcy," she muttered, nervously fingering the napkin in her lap.

"Have you known him long?"

She shook her head. "I met him after coming to St. Augustine. He's here supervising the construction of a hotel on the island." Her voice was low, and she shivered involuntarily.

Lloyd was observing her curiously. "Well, he's certainly made an impression on you. You look positively devastated."

"I can't understand what he's doing here," she said, a despairing note creeping into her voice.

"He's not staying at the Monterey?"

Brook put one elbow on the table, shielding her eyes with her hand. "No. He has a yacht in the harbor."

Lloyd's shaggy brows rose. "I see. Then it's rather obvious what he's doing here, isn't it? He must have come to see you, but when he saw that you were with me, he changed his mind. I don't like that look on his face, if you want to know the truth."

Brook managed a faint smile. "Neither do I." She drew a deep breath. "Lloyd, I want to go back to my room. You stay if you want to."

"Do you think I'd let you go alone, the way you're looking?" He signaled the waiter for their check. "I'll see you to your door."

When they reached her room, he said, "Brook,

this is none of my business, but it's obvious something has been going on here between you and this Darcy. I've just remembered that I've heard his name before. He's a big man in these parts, as I recall, and something of a connoisseur of women. I really don't think he's your type." He surveyed her unhappy countenance. "You're too good for some furtive affair."

She responded softly, "Lloyd, I agree with you." She touched his arm affectionately. "You don't have to worry about me." She unlocked her door and stepped inside.

Lloyd thrust his head in to say, "I'll check on you later. Call my room if you need anything."

She nodded before closing and locking the door, then leaned back against it, seeing Dane's tense face again. He had looked furious, and that baffled her. Had he really come to the Monterey to see her? She couldn't understand it, so she tried to forget it. After bathing and getting into a gown and robe, she found one of the paperback novels she'd brought with her and sat down on the couch to read.

A few minutes later, there was a knock at her door. Lloyd, she thought, smiling. Bless his fatherly heart. She laid her book aside and padded barefoot to the door.

She barely had it open when it was shoved back and Dane strode grimly into the room. Brook tensed, watching his hard profile as he turned to face her.

"Shut the door," he commanded.

She felt cold rushing over her skin. "Not until you're on the other side of it."

Cursing, he took a few steps and slammed the door shut with a bang.

"Please, Dane," she quivered.

"Why did you lie to Amanda?" His dark eyes held hers almost hypnotically, boring into hers.

Brook ran a tongue over her lips. "I've never lied to her!"

"You told her yesterday that you were leaving St. Augustine today," he snapped.

"Oh—and how did you know I hadn't?"

"I phoned the hotel and asked," he retorted. "That's why I'm here, and I want an answer."

Her eyes tried to slide away from him, but she seemed to have lost control of her movements. "I planned to leave today. But Lloyd Pennington, the author of the book I'm illustrating, called last night to say he'd be here today to go over my sketches."

"Pennington?" he said tautly. "Is that the bearded character I saw you with before?"

"Yes," she said huskily.

His mouth curved mockingly. "You've certainly been busy since you left the yacht, haven't you? Juggling dates with Alex Revard and your writer friend. My God, you can switch your affection with unbelievable ease! Pennington just arrived and already the two of you have gotten damned cozy. Where is he now? Hiding in the bathroom?"

Her face washed a hot, angry red. "You have a nerve, questioning me! I don't care what you think of me, Dane, but just to set the record straight, Lloyd has a wife and children whom he adores. He isn't like you. He doesn't try to get every woman he sees into bed."

He stared at her angrily. "Give me one good reason why I ought to believe you. I'm not as easily duped as Alex."

"You haven't the common decency that Alex has, either! Oh—believe what you want. Just get out of here."

"Decency has nothing to do with what Alex wants from you. I watched the two of you together the day of the picnic. I didn't get the impression he was interested in anything but getting you in the sack."

"Oh, *please,*" Brook moaned, dropping her face into her hands. "Leave me alone, Dane."

He caught her wrists, forcing her hands away from her face. Then he wrenched her toward him and she cried out at the implacability she saw in the obsidian depths of his eyes. In her struggle to be free, her body arched against him, and she saw a flicker of arousal in his face.

He bent his head until his mouth was almost touching hers. "I want you more than they do," he whispered hoarsely.

"Don't," pleaded Brook in a trembling voice, staring back at him with fearful eyes.

His hand curved around her neck, and she shivered as his warm fingers slowly caressed it. "For years you've gotten away with promising men more than you are willing to deliver—McAnnally, Alex, Pennington, and Lord knows how many others. Oh, maybe you don't do it intentionally, but there is a silent invitation in the way you've looked at me sometimes, and I'm not so stupid as to believe I'm unique. Only this time it's backfired, hasn't it? You respond to me whether you want to or not."

Her eyes widened in confusion. She knew that what Dane said contained some truth. She had always known just how far to let a man go before she pulled away. She'd never thought of it as leading men on; but she had been very careful to keep an impenetrable barrier about herself and her emotions. Somehow Dane Darcy had battered down that barrier and made her feel needs and desires that dazzled and bewildered her.

154

He gave her a long glance. "I have an advantage the others didn't have, and I intend to use it."

"What—do you mean?"

He smiled before his mouth closed the tiny space separating it from hers in a possessive, demanding kiss. She heard the muffled thudding of his heart as his arms tightened around her, pulling her urgently against him. His need communicated itself to her as if there were no barriers of clothing and skin separating them. Her body began to tremble. She fought against the sensual impact he was having on her, but his strong hands were traveling up and down her back, molding her closer to him.

"No, Dane," she moaned against his lips. But he only deepened the kiss, drawing out the sweet arousal until her lips parted, became softly yielding as she began to kiss him back and her arms went around his neck. Dimly she realized that this was where she had wanted to be, locked in his embrace, since the first time she saw him. She craved the feel of his body, his kisses, as a starving person craved food.

Reason deserted her and she yielded to her feelings, her hands stroking the strong column of his neck, her mouth exploring the wonders of his with a demand as urgent as his own. Dane's heartbeat quickened as he felt her yield and, gently, he pressed her back until she was lying across the bed. He lay half across her as he opened her robe and urgent fingers pushed the straps of her gown off her shoulders, pulling the thin material down to expose her breasts. Already the rosy peaks were thrusting rigidly with the need that coursed through her body. He bent his head to trail kisses down her neck and across her shoulder to the swelling, silken skin of her breast. Her fingers entangled themselves in the hair at the back of his neck, and she pressed him closer to her body. His mouth captured one taut peak, surrounding it with moist heat that caused her to turn her head from side to side in a wild abandonment that she had never known before. A hoarsely incoherent moan escaped her.

"Tell me that you want me, too," he muttered thickly. "Tell me, Brook."

"Yes—" she gasped weakly, for she had gone too far for denial.

He breathed a low sigh of satisfaction and his hold on her lightened while his mouth continued its hot exploration. His hand trailed lightly down her body, molding itself to the contours of her breast, then tracing her slender waist and coming to rest warmly on her stomach.

Impatient to be closer to him, she fumbled at the buttons of his shirt, sliding her hands inside to stroke the rough mat of hair on his hard chest and explore the broad, muscled expanse of his back.

When the bedside phone rang shrilly near her head, for several seconds she could not make her brain function, and the phone had rung a number of times before she could overcome her dazed senses enough to move.

"Dane—"

He lifted his head to look into her heavy-lidded eyes. "Let it ring."

She swallowed, feeling as if she were drowning in the dilated depths of his dark eyes. The raging heat inside her body had not subsided, and she felt utterly shaken by what he had aroused in her.

"I—I have to answer it," she whispered through lips that tingled from his assault on them. "It's probably Lloyd, and if I don't answer he'll come to see why."

She lay beneath him, breathing heavily as he

stared down at her. Then, abruptly, he sat up, lifted the receiver from its cradle and handed it to her.

She gripped the plastic hardness and, oddly, the simple presence of that common instrument of everyday life forced reality, harsh and unadorned, upon her. She understood now what she was capable of when she let all the barriers down. There was no question as to what would have happened, had the ringing of the telephone not jarred into her drugged state.

"Hello," she said softly.

"Brook, were you asleep?" Lloyd Pennington's voice rumbled over the wire. "You don't sound like yourself. Is anything wrong?"

She didn't feel like herself, either, she thought with irony. "No—I wasn't asleep."

"I thought I ought to tell you something," he went on. "After I left you I went down to the bar. I saw Darcy getting into the elevator. I thought he might be coming up to your room."

She was silent for a moment. "Don't worry about me, Lloyd."

"Listen, you don't sound right. I'm coming up there to see for myself."

"That isn't necessary—" But he had already hung up.

She replaced the receiver and sat up on the side of the bed. Dane had gotten to his feet and was standing beside her, looking down at her. A wry smile touched his lips as his gaze swept over her. "You're beautiful."

Belatedly, she became aware that her breasts, still swollen and tender from his touch, were fully exposed to his view. She looked away from him in confusion, flushing hotly, and quickly pulled her robe together to cover herself.

157

He laughed softly. "You look intoxicated. What are you thinking?"

"That you'd better go," she whispered. "Lloyd is on his way up here."

She saw a tightening of his jaw. "Do you want me to come back?" he asked shortly, watching her.

She tried to speak with conviction. "No. I don't want to see you again, Dane."

He stared at her for another long moment. "As you wish," he said through his teeth. He turned and left quickly, and she did not watch him go.

She went into the bathroom to straighten her clothing and smooth her hair and otherwise try to bring some semblance of order to her appearance. It was not so easy to bring order to her thoughts. She stared into her flushed face, wondering how she could have lost all pride and dignity in the space of a few minutes. Dane could have done anything to her and she would not have protested. She could no longer deny the terrible hold he had on her. Dear heaven, she *was* in love with him—desperately, hopelessly. And after he had told her he would never love again. He hadn't tried to deceive her where his own feelings were concerned, and she was every kind of a fool to have permitted what had happened with him tonight.

She turned away from her own strained face as she heard Lloyd at the door, calling her name.

He walked into the room, studied her thoughtfully for a moment, then glanced about. "He was here, wasn't he?"

"Yes," she admitted, "but everything's all right."

He shook his head in disbelief. "How can you stand there with that stricken look on your face and say everything is all right?"

She sighed tiredly and moved to the couch, where she sat and stared at her hands folded in her lap.

"I've got a mighty broad shoulder," Lloyd told her, "and I'm a good listener."

She shook her head. "You're a good friend, Lloyd, but I don't want to burden you with my problems."

He sat down beside her, a look of concern bringing his shaggy brows together. "Are you in love with him?"

She took a shaky breath. "I—I suppose I am. But I'm just another woman to him. That's why I can't—well, give my feelings free rein. Do you understand?"

He gave a short laugh. "Perfectly." He scanned her face. "You're in love with him, all right. Is that why you were in such a hurry to leave St. Augustine?"

She nodded wordlessly, and he went on, "If you don't think you can stay—"

"No," she cut him off, lifting her chin. "I'll stay until the job's done."

"It'll only take a few days. And if you should find yourself in another difficult situation with Darcy, you know you can call on me for help—if you really want it, that is."

She smiled ruefully. "Thanks, Lloyd."

He got to his feet. "I'll let you get to bed now. Don't forget. Call me anytime—even if you just feel like talking."

"I will," she promised.

When he was gone, she sat for a long time with her head in her hands, her aching heart mocking her.

Chapter Nine

She was dragged reluctantly from sleep at six the next morning. Groaning a protest, she lifted her wrist and peered at her watch, wondering what had awakened her. Then there was a loud knock at her door and Lloyd's voice calling, "Brook, I have to talk to you."

She yawned sleepily and threw back the sheet, fumbling for her robe as she got out of bed. Tying the sash with fingers as sluggish as her brain, she opened the door a crack. "I'm *not* going to start work this early, Lloyd!"

"I'm sorry to have to wake you, but I have to go back home. May I come in for a minute?" His usually unflappable manner was missing. He seemed disturbed.

She stood back while he entered. "It's Jack," he told her, "my oldest boy. They've taken him to the hospital and he's scheduled for an emergency appendectomy at seven. Kim is beside herself. Her mother had to stay at home with the other kids. I have to get there to be with Kim as soon as I can."

"That's terrible, Lloyd! Of course, you have to be there. How soon can you get a flight?"

"Eight-thirty." He ran a hand over his beard. "Jack's never complained of pain in his abdomen— If I'd had any idea—"

"Don't start blaming yourself for being away from home when this happened."

"I'm not. I'm just trying to take it in, I guess. Jack's only twelve."

"And strong and healthy," Brook reminded him.

"Sure. You're right." He pulled a sheet of paper from his shirt pocket. "I've made a detailed list of the new sketches I want you to do. I feel rotten, running out on you like this, but—"

"Don't be silly." Brook took the list, scanning it. "I can handle it. Oh—" She handed him a bulging folder from the couch. "You can take your manuscript with you. I've finished reading it."

His smile was grateful. "There's no great rush about the new sketches. When you've finished, mail all the illustrations to my editor. If we need a three-way meeting after that, we can get in touch with you. And thanks for being so understanding."

"You're welcome," she told him, giving him a gentle shove. "Now get out of here—and try not to worry. An appendectomy is really a routine operation."

"I know. I'm worried as much about Kim, in her condition, as I am about Jack."

Brook closed the door behind him and went back to bed. But her mind was too occupied with the Penningtons' emergency for her to sleep. Finally she got dressed and went down for breakfast soon after the coffee shop opened at seven.

She took her supplies with her, planning to leave

directly after breakfast for her day's work. If she put in long hours, she might do all the sketches on Lloyd's list in two days.

She'd finished eating and was having a second cup of coffee when the sound of a familiar voice brought her head up with a jerk. Dane was standing beside her table.

"I'm glad I caught you before you left the hotel."

She blinked her eyes, trying to ignore her leaping pulses. "You just barely did." She picked up her check and her bulging straw bag and stood. "In fact, I was about to go."

His hand on her arm detained her, and she looked up at him, her eyes widening. "Let go of me, Dane."

"Where's your writer friend?"

"He was called home unexpectedly." She took a step away from him.

"Please, Brook, give me a minute of your time."

Since she didn't want to draw attention to herself by struggling to free herself from his hold, she said curtly, "What do you want?"

"To apologize for last night. I think I came on too strong, and I'm sorry."

She stared into his eyes and wondered what he was really thinking. His tone and expression seemed to be sincere. "All right." The words were clipped. "You weren't entirely to blame, after all."

He grinned wickedly. "I did have a little help, didn't I?"

In the cold light of a new day, Brook, unlike Dane, could find nothing amusing in what had happened between them last night. "I accept your apology," she said curtly. "Now, good-bye."

His hand on her arm tightened and his grin vanished. "I'm not finished." A trace of impatience edged the tone now. "Will you let me make it up to you?"

"I ~~hardly~~ see how you can do that," she said, her voice dry.

"I don't want your last memory of me to be tainted." She suspected there was mockery in the statement, but his blue-black eyes looked back at her with a directness that seemed utterly honest. "I'd be grateful if you would spend the day with me."

She made a humorless sound. "Aboard the Aphrodite, I suppose. What have you done with Amanda and Rosa? Locked them in their staterooms?"

She saw his nostrils flare slightly. "Not aboard the Aphrodite. I'd like to take you up to St. Simon's Island. It's just over the state line in Georgia, but not a long drive."

"Dane," she snapped, "what's all this about?"

"I told you," he replied stubbornly, "I want to leave you with pleasant memories of me. I want to prove to you that I can behave as properly as Alex Revard or any other man."

Her doubtful look was apparently not lost on him, for he changed the subject. "Have you been to St. Simon's before?" He was staring down at her with a determined glint in his eyes.

"Do you really think I'm naive enough," she said heatedly, "to believe your reason for taking a day off work—when I know you have deadlines to meet—is to impress me with your propriety? It's a bit too late for that!"

"I don't expect you to believe it now, but you will by the time the day's over." He paused, then added coaxingly, "It would only delay your work one day. If I can leave mine that long, surely you can."

Brook glanced about, noticing that several of the tables had been filled since she had entered. "Dane, will you let go of me? People are beginning to stare."

Without releasing her, he pulled a bill from his pocket with his free hand, snatched her breakfast

163

check from her hand, and tossed both on the table. Then, still clutching her upper arm, he propelled her toward the hotel foyer. "We'll go where we can talk more privately," he informed her.

As usual, she thought angrily, he didn't bother to ask how she felt about a private talk.

When he had her trapped in a corner of the deserted foyer, he went on, "The most beautiful old church you've ever seen is on St. Simon's. You'll have plenty of time to make sketches. Believe me, you'll thank me when you see it. The whole island is steeped in American history. And one of the best restaurants in the country is at the entrance to the causeway that leads to St. Simon's. We'll have dinner there." Steel determination was in every line of him. Well, hadn't he told her he usually got what he wanted?

Brook caught her bottom lip between her teeth uncertainly. Last night she had convinced herself that she never wanted to see Dane again. But now, as he stood only inches away, his long lean body clad in tight, white duck trousers and a brown open-necked sport shirt, she could not deny the fluttering response of her heart nor the part of her that had wanted to acquiesce to his demand all along.

Now that Lloyd was gone, a day lost from her assignment was of no real consequence. Was it so wrong to want to spend one more day with Dane, when it would probably be the last time she ever saw him?

He must have sensed that her resistance was weakening, for he said quickly, "We can visit the remains of the English village of Frederica, too. It was built in the early 1700's. Part of the old fort is still there, and you can see the layout of the entire town. At one time it was one of the most important towns in the British colony of Georgia."

"I—I'd have to be back before too late."

"Done." He smiled crookedly, charmingly, now that he had gotten his way. "The car's just outside the door. Do you need to get anything from your room before we go?"

She shook her head and, as he steered her toward the foyer doors, she stifled a sudden rush of second thoughts. Already she was eager to see the things he had mentioned, but even stronger was the desire, in spite of her nagging better judgment, to grab these final hours with Dane.

Neither of them spoke until they were on the coastal highway, the Cadillac eating up the miles smoothly and noiselessly. She had chosen to wear sturdy walking shorts and a sleeveless knit shirt for what she had expected to be a long work day. She might have dressed more carefully had she known what the day held in store for her. She sighed inwardly, deciding that it really didn't matter, anyway. Dane had seen her in hardly anything at all. At this point, it would be useless to try to put on a more sophisticated exterior.

Dane glanced over at her. "Why was Pennington called home?"

"His son's having an emergency appendectomy this morning." She continued to gaze through the windshield, stifling a desire to glance over at him to let her eyes take in enough visual memories to last a lifetime. She wasn't likely ever to forget a single thing about Dane Darcy, at any rate. "His wife's pregnant and, in addition to worrying about his son, he's concerned about how she is taking it."

"How many children does he have?"

"Four."

A low chuckle escaped him. "And another on the way? Sounds as if he's been very busy at home. I

165

guess I really was wrong about Pennington's having designs on you."

"You certainly were." She flicked a look at him then, met his narrowed eyes for a moment. "You've been wrong about almost everything where I'm concerned, but I really don't want to discuss it."

"Okay," he retorted good-naturedly. "By the way, Tanya let something slip the last time I saw her that you should know about. It seems she phoned McAnnally and told him some cock-and-bull story to get him down here."

Brook leaned back against the comfortable seat, half closing her eyes. "I know all about that."

His glance was sharp. "Why in hell didn't you tell me then, when I was giving you such a hard time over McAnnally's turning up at the yacht?"

She shot him an ironic look. "I didn't see what could be accomplished by telling you, except to make you angry with Tanya."

He shook his head in puzzlement. "I was angry, all right! I almost strangled her. I've been trying to get Tanya out of my hair without being unnecessarily cruel, but after I forced her to admit what she'd done, I didn't worry about insulting her anymore."

Brook shifted uneasily against the seat. "I don't want to be the cause of any—problems between you and Tanya."

"Brook." His hand reached out to touch her chin, forcing it up so that she had to look at him. "Have you been imagining that Tanya has some importance in my life?"

"I—I just assumed—"

"Tanya doesn't mean a thing to me, she never has. Whatever assumptions you have made to the contrary are quite wrong." He let go of her chin and returned his hand to the wheel. She remembered that day at Fort Caroline when Tanya had told her she and Dane planned a Christmas wedding. The woman had been lying. But, of course, Brook had wondered about that at the time.

"Apparently," she murmured, "there have been some false assumptions on both sides."

He gave her another quick look, then turned his attention to the road, uttering an uncommunicative grunt. After a few moments, he switched on the radio for a news report, and Brook was glad for the sound of the commentator's voice, which made further conversation unnecessary.

When they reached St. Simon's, Dane drove first to the state park that was the site of the former English village, Frederica. They toured the museum, standing for a good while beside a scale model of the town as it had looked in its heyday.

"Frederica was General Oglethorpe's military headquarters for operations against the Spanish in Florida," Dane told her. "There was a regiment of over five hundred men stationed here. At the time, this land was claimed by Britain, France, and Spain."

Having just made the rather short drive to St. Simon's, Brook could understand that the Spanish to the south must have felt threatened by a British military post so close to them. "Did the Spanish try to drive them out?"

"Oh, they tried," Dane said. "In 1739 there was a series of skirmishes that came to be called the War of Jenkins' Ear, in honor of a British soldier whose ear was cut off by the Spaniards."

Brook laughed at his serious expression. "You're kidding."

"It's true," he told her. "Check any history book. Anyway, the war culminated with the Battle of

Bloody Marsh on St. Simon's where the Spanish were defeated. They lost two hundred men; the British lost only poor Jenkins' ear.''

They left the museum to wander through the town site which overlooked the Frederica River. The settlers, Dane explained, were chosen carefully according to the duties they could perform, so that the colony could be self-sufficient and self-supporting. Home sites of the shoemaker, dyer, chandler, baker, tanner, coachman, carpenter, bricklayer, miller, accountant, surveyor, and doctor were marked with tiny plaques. All that remained now were a few crumbling foundation stones, but they were enough to allow visitors to imagine what the town must have been like in the 1700s.

Brook made a quick sketch of the remains of the fort before they returned to the car to drive to Christ Church.

As they drove slowly down the tree-lined lane near the church, they saw a number of cars parked alongside and the occupants entering or leaving the large, walled yard. "The church is as much of a tourist attraction as Frederica," Dane observed.

As the gracious white structure came into view, Brook could understand why, and she caught her breath in admiration. Nestled in a huge expanse of lush, green lawn and surrounded by ancient live oak trees dripping Spanish moss, Christ Church had a trussed Gothic roof with a cross-topped steeple in front of many tall, stained glass windows. Those windows that reflected the afternoon sun depicted scenes in the life of Christ in brilliant, glowing hues.

Dane looked at her, smiling at the awed expression on her face. "Do you like it?"

"Need you ask?" Brook breathed. "It's too beautiful to be real! It looks like a painting. Oh, I want to make some sketches."

"I knew you would," he said resignedly. They got out and strolled toward the wide-open gate in the stone wall that marked the outer perimeter of the churchyard. "I'll leave you alone for a while," he went on and as they passed through the gate he ambled toward the small cemetery that was a part of the churchyard.

Brook went inside the church where an elderly woman was telling a group of visitors something of Christ Church's history. The original church, she said, had been built by plantation owners in 1808, but it was looted and destroyed during the Civil War. Union troops camped inside, broke the windows, burned the pews for firewood, and used the building as a slaughtering house for butchering cattle. The church was restored by a member of an early St. Simon's family as a memorial to his wife, Ellen, who had died while they were in India on their honeymoon. Ellen's body was buried in a vault beneath the chancel of the church and remained there until her husband's death, at which time the two were placed in a joint grave in the churchyard cemetery.

Outside again, Brook sat down on the thick, cushiony grass in an out-of-the-way corner of the yard and began to sketch the church, pausing now and then for long moments just to gaze at the serene green-and-white loveliness all around her. In spite of the trickle of tourists coming and going, the place exuded a peace so profound that she felt almost as if she could reach out and touch it. It gave her the feeling of having stepped back into an earlier, slower-paced era. She thought about the young bride, Ellen, and her grieving young husband and wondered fancifully if their spirits watched over the old church.

She was finishing her third sketch from another spot on the lawn when Dane strolled up to look over her shoulder. The previous two sketches lay on the grass beside her. He bent to pick them up and studied them silently.

"These are excellent," he murmured finally.

Brook looked up to smile at him. "Would you like one? You may take your pick."

He studied the sketches again, then chose the first one she'd done. "I like the angle of this one. Thank you, Brook. I'll treasure this."

Their gazes held for a moment, and Brook felt a rush of color in her cheeks and the feeling that Dane had always aroused in her, warmth invading all her veins. She returned the two sketches Dane hadn't chosen along with her pad and pencil to her bag, then took his hand, proffered to help her to her feet. They walked toward the Cadillac, her hand still clasped warmly in his. She didn't try to pull away. It felt too good to have him touching her for her to consider that.

In the car, she said, "Where is this restaurant you've been raving about? I'm starving." They had stopped at a roadside stand for lunch, but Brook had only had a glass of juice.

Dane started the engine and pulled back into the lane. "We have one more stop to make before we leave the island, if you think you can wait a bit longer. I want to show you the old lighthouse. It's still in use, by the way, but the keeper's cottage has been turned into a museum of coastal history."

"Umm," she agreed. "I wouldn't want to miss that." She put her head back against the seat and gazed out the side window at close-growing trees in a wilderness area and, later, houses set back from the road in green lawns.

They spent a half hour in the small museum, then stopped for a few minutes on the cliff overlooking the Atlantic Ocean. They left the island on King's Way, crossing the causeway to the mainland where Dane turned the car into a parking area already nearly filled with cars.

"Emmeline and Hessie's," Dane told her as they walked toward the rustic, wood-and-glass restaurant that extended out over the water.

"Judging from all the cars, it must have a good reputation."

"The best," Dane said. "It's known all over this part of the country."

At Dane's request, they were given a table next to a window looking out on the water. The interior of the large restaurant consisted of wood panels alternating with great panes of glass. There were high, slanting ceiling beams and planters of greenery everywhere. All the waitresses seemed to be attractive, smiling college-age girls, certainly a fine advertisement for the place.

Their meal consisted of french fried mushroom appetizers, baked shrimp stuffed with crabmeat and served with whole wheat muffins, and English trifles for dessert. It was, indeed, one of the more delicious meals Brook had ever eaten.

Their appetites sated, they lingered over brandies and coffee, talking and watching darkness come in over the water. Brook wished fleetingly that she could stop time at that moment, remain always in that dimly lighted intimacy with Dane.

"I'm putting Amanda in a new school next term," he told her. "Along with good instruction in the basics, they emphasize the fine arts. Thanks to your guidance while you were with us, she's decided she wants to take art lessons. Of course, part of the school's attraction is the fact that her friend, Linda, goes there."

"That sounds like a good idea," Brook said. "It's a private school?"

He nodded. "Uniforms and the whole bit. The place has a first-rate reputation. They keep the classes small and try to give individual attention." He sipped his coffee, adding, "They also have a limousine service to pick up the students at home and deliver them after school."

"That eases my mind," Brook said and he looked over at her in surprise. "I know about the kidnap attempt," she went on. "Alex told me that day on the yacht."

"You haven't mentioned it to Amanda, have you?"

She shook her head and Dane continued, "It's just that I'm not sure she was old enough to understand what was happening at the time. She's never talked about it, and I've not wanted to frighten her by explaining what was really taking place. I managed to keep it out of the papers. That kind of publicity might have given some other nut ideas. When she's a little older, I'll talk to her about the necessity of caution for a child of mine." He grimaced slightly. "It isn't a very pleasant thing to have to tell your daughter."

"It isn't, is it?" Brook agreed. "But Amanda's pretty strong emotionally; so I don't think you need to worry about talking to her and telling her to take precautions." A soft smile touched her lips. "You know, I didn't realize how hard it would be to tell Amanda good-bye until the time came. She couldn't understand why I didn't stay on in St. Augustine indefinitely. At any rate, she pretended that she didn't. Frankly, I think she hasn't enough to do and she's getting bored."

"I've come to the same conclusion. I've decided to

send Rosa and Amanda back to Miami if I can't wrap up this job in two or three weeks. At home she has her own things and her friends, at least, and I can probably get down there on most weekends."

"It hasn't been easy for you, raising Amanda alone," Brook said. "I'm afraid I didn't understand for a while how much you really do care for her."

He shrugged. "As you said this morning, there have been some false assumptions on both sides." The way he was looking at her caused her heart to turn over. She sipped her coffee in an attempt to dislodge the sudden swelling in her throat. Oh, God, how she loved him! And she had to stop! It was a futile love that could only hurt her.

Dane had leaned forward, reaching across the table to capture her hand. "Brook," he said quietly, "before Amanda returns to Miami I'm considering taking the yacht to the Bahamas for a few days of relaxation. Will you come with us?"

She gazed at the tanned, angled planes of his face, feeling an impulse to reach out and trace the hard cheekbone and jaw, to touch the firm line of his lips. Dear heaven, how she would adore going to the Bahamas with Dane. But she knew that things had already gone too far for her to be able to stay out of his bed during another stay on the yacht. And when it was over, the parting would devastate her.

"I can't," she said huskily.

"It would make Amanda happy," he responded hopefully.

She moved her hand from under his, dropping it into her lap. "That isn't fair, Dane. You know how fond I am of Amanda, and you're using that to try to manipulate me. But I can't be Amanda's mother figure. I can't go with you. I—I have work to do."

His eyes narrowed on her face. "You don't trust

yourself with me anymore, do you? You're afraid of what might happen if we're together for several days."

She lifted her chin, meeting his look. "Maybe I am. We would only hurt each other, Dane. I—I'm not sure I could deal with that. These past few weeks have been an interlude, nothing more. I have to go on with my life now."

His eyes probed her face in a silent search for something that, apparently, they did not find, for he suggested that they leave without further delay. In the car, moving through the darkness, Dane switched on the radio, as if he didn't care to talk. That was just as well, Brook thought, for she didn't know what else the two of them had to say to each other.

She half expected him to drop her at the front entrance of the hotel and speed off into the night. But he pulled into a parking space and got out to see her to her room. She wanted to tell him not to come, but she knew it would do no good, so she walked beside him in heavy silence until they reached her door.

She spoke for the first time in several minutes. "I enjoyed the day very much. Thank you."

His gaze ran down the soft curves of her slender body, his eyes wry. "Can't wait to be rid of me?"

"I—I didn't mean—"

He smiled dryly. "What didn't you mean?"

She looked up into the blue-black eyes and her heart plunged helplessly. She glanced away, swallowing, feeling herself begin to quake inside.

He moved, pulling her into his arms, and his mouth found hers with a dizzying insistence that silenced and shattered her. As his tongue parted her lips, she felt all her defenses crumbling. Oh, God, it wasn't fair—it wasn't fair for one human being to have this kind of hold on another. After long moments he released her mouth to trail gentle butterfly kisses along her jaw line and down to the pulse that beat so wildly at the base of her throat. Her body, as if with a will of its own, molded its softness against the hard length of his, and her hands gripped his shoulders with a feverish need.

He groaned softly against her throat. "Let me come in with you."

But she knew what would happen then, knew and both wanted it and despised herself for the wanting. Somehow she had to find the strength to send him away. His questing lips had followed the low vee of her blouse to the warm valley between her breasts, and a tiny moan of pleasure escaped her. Hearing, she wondered for one confused moment who had made the sound, then realized that it was herself. It was madness to allow herself to feel this way about a man like Dane Darcy. He had lifted his head and his eyes rested on her mouth. "Well?"

Her knees went weak at the passionate look he gave her, but she had always been one to weigh things carefully before following a potential course of action to its ultimate conclusion. Fortunately that tendency, though wavering, didn't desert her now.

"No, Dane."

He watched her face intently. "When are you going home?"

"In two or three days."

"May I see you again before you go?"

Aware of the injured glitter in the dark eyes, she stepped out of his arms. "I—I think it would be better if we don't see each other again."

He pushed his hands into his pockets. "Not better for me," he said flatly.

Trembling, she found her door key in the straw bag and looked up at him again, her mouth dry. "Dane—oh, Dane, it's better for both of us."

He stood still. "Do you really mean that?" His face was pale underneath the tan.

It was a great effort to push the word out. "Yes."

He looked a little dazed as he continued to stare at her. Then his face darkened. "Good night."

She watched him walking down the hall away from her until he had turned the corner and was out of sight. As she stepped inside her dark room, the snap of the door closing behind her sounded loud and final in the silence. A sob of searing regret escaped her. She felt such utter desolation, and every nerve in her body seemed to be jerking, as if she might fly apart at any moment.

Dane had warned her that love brought more pain than it was worth, and he was right.

Chapter Ten

Over the next three days, her mood was disconsolate most of the time. She couldn't seem to keep herself from asking at the hotel desk whenever she came in if there had been any messages for her. The answer was always the same: "No messages, Miss Adamson."

"Well, that's that," she told herself. "He's not going to try to see me again. It's what I want, isn't it?"

Lloyd had called the day after her trip to St. Simon's to tell her that both Jack and Kim were recovering nicely from the surgery. "I can't see much point in coming back down there now," he said. "You really don't need me, do you?"

"I hate to deflate your ego," Brook quipped, "but I'm doing remarkably well on my own. You're going to be pleased with the new sketches, I think."

"I'm sure of it," Lloyd agreed. "How about that other problem? You bearing up okay?"

"Couldn't be better."

But whenever she looked at herself in the mirror, she noticed that her face had a weary pallor despite her suntanned skin.

The quaint atmosphere of the old town could still envelop her in its attraction for brief periods, and she spent as much time there as she could. Not as much as she would have liked, though, since most of the sketches Lloyd wanted were at other sites.

Alex Revard phoned one evening to invite her to dinner, but she refused. They had nothing in common, really, and she didn't feel up to trying to carry her end of a conversation with him. Brook had had enough of encounters with men for a good long while. Alex was a nice man, and she liked him, but she wanted nothing to do with any man.

On the third day, when she finished the final sketches on Lloyd's list, she arranged for a noon flight from Jacksonville to Kansas City the next day, then located a car rental agency that would deliver a car to her hotel early the next morning and allow her to leave it at the Jacksonville airport.

Everything was tidily arranged for her departure, except that she was leaving a part of herself behind, for she had changed in subtle ways. Never again would she be so quick to condemn other women who remained in destructive relationships with men. Never again would she be quite so sure of her own invulnerability.

When she stowed her bags in the trunk and got into the rental car on the morning of her departure, she contemplated the drive ahead of her with relief. She still had a full week before she had to begin a new assignment, and she was feeling homesick for Kansas City and her own apartment. She would spend the coming week relaxing, visiting with her parents, and replenishing her art supplies and her wardrobe for the assignment, which fortunately was within daily driving distance of Kansas City. She could return to her own apartment at night.

She felt the need now, as she hadn't in a long time, of knowing that her parents were nearby. She had no intention of confiding in them the changes that had been wrought in her while in St. Augustine, but knowing she could see them whenever she wanted gave her a little added feeling of security. This thought brought a wry smile to her lips.

"You're a little young yet to be in your second childhood, Brook," she chided herself as she drove the rental car away from the Monterey and headed north toward Jacksonville.

Arriving at the airport, she checked her one large bag through, then bought a magazine and went to the coffee shop to pass the hour until it would be time to go to the boarding gate. She had worn the white silk tunic and slacks and, as she passed a mirror behind the coffee shop cashier's desk, she noticed with satisfaction the attractive contrast the white made with her Florida tan. The tan was, she told herself, at least one nice thing she was taking home with her. "Let us count our blessings," she murmured to herself. "Lord knows they are pretty scarce right now."

She slid into a vacant booth, ordered coffee, and opened the fashion magazine to scan several designers' summer offerings. It looked as if white was definitely in this season and, if she could only find the time to maintain her tan during the summer, the new fashions would be flattering.

She finished the magazine with a good forty-five minutes to spare before she went to the gate. Sighing, she ordered more coffee and sat back to study her fellow customers in the coffee shop.

There was a bustle about an airport that was not

quite like any other. People looked at their watches more frequently and their conversations seemed, from outward appearances, more intense, as if they were determined to say all that they might ever want to say to the person they would be parting from when their flight was called. Brook was glad that she wasn't carrying on one of those parting conversations and could relax without talking. She had already made her goodbyes to Rosa and Amanda—and to Dane.

She definitely did not like the direction her thoughts were taking and, giving herself a mental shake, glanced toward the cashier's desk and the entry door. Just as she did so, a tall broad-shouldered form in a beige summer suit appeared in the open doorway, frowning and looking over the customers in the coffee shop intently.

Brook felt her face changing from relaxation to tenseness as she recognized Dane. A painful constriction tightened her throat, and she felt as if she were frozen to her seat. Dane's roving glance settled on her then, and she saw something like relief in his face as he pushed through a knot of customers waiting at the cashier's desk to pay their checks and came toward her.

Her hands gripped her handbag, which lay in her lap, as if she meant to use it as a shield. Nervously she watched Dane's approach. He stopped beside her table, looking down at her.

"May I sit down?"

Brook hesitated, but could find no excuse for refusing, so she nodded wordlessly. Dane sat across from her, looking dark and handsome, his blond head turning to glance once more about the room. Then he turned back to her with a slight smile.

"Can I buy you another cup of coffee?"

She gave him a harassed, uncomprehending look. "No, thank you. I've already had two."

With apparent calm, he lifted a hand to motion a waitress to the table and ordered coffee for himself. Then he proceeded to add cream and stir slowly before lifting the cup to his mouth.

It crossed her mind that she should not say anything until he did. Perhaps the silence would make him as uncomfortable as she felt. But she knew that it wouldn't, and her anxiety loosened her tongue. "Why are you here, Dane?" She looked down at her hands, still clutching her handbag.

He did not answer immediately, and she lifted her head to look at him. The bones under the deep tan of his face seemed to harden as he met her glance. For the first time, she saw that he looked rather haggard; there were dark hollows under his eyes.

"I can't let you go," he said huskily.

Brook's hands shook. Carefully, she placed her handbag on the seat beside her and clasped her hands together, as if she had to hold on to herself to keep from shaking apart.

He was sitting rigidly, staring at her intensely, his blue-black eyes filled with a pain that she had never perceived in them.

"Don't do this," she muttered, looking away. Was this the latest manipulation, the ultimate attempt to get what he wanted from her? Unknowingly, she had shrunk back in a corner of the booth away from him.

"I won't try to touch you," Dane said harshly. "I've been fighting this out with myself for days—for weeks, actually—and I know now that you won't be any more likely to be convinced if I use strength to get you in my arms."

Unable to keep looking into the pain in his eyes, she leaned forward to put her elbows on the table and bury her face in her hands. "Why," she whispered brokenly, "must you make this more difficult for me than it already is?"

"Because I love you." The words sounded as if they had been wrenched forcibly from the deepest recesses of his soul. The trembling in her body increased, and she kept her face averted, listening as he continued speaking in that driven way. She had never heard him speak in such deadly earnest before.

"I think it started the first time I saw you. I didn't understand why your innocent trespassing and, later, your coming to Amanda's birthday dinner made me so angry. I only knew that you were dangerous for me—dangerous because you made me feel things I never wanted to feel again."

She lifted her head slowly, looking at him with searching incredulity. He stared at her, his dark eyes deep and vulnerable, his hands clenched tightly together on the tabletop as though he were on the point of violence. "I was even jealous of poor Alex Revard, an old friend! I couldn't stand watching him look at you." His mouth twisted with his pent-up frustrations. "I tried to make myself believe you were like other women I'd known, the sort of woman who would use a child to get an invitation aboard my yacht, a woman who would use her looks to get the security and the luxuries that a rich husband, or even a rich lover, could provide."

Brook grimaced bitterly. "I know what you thought of me. You told me every chance you got."

His eyes probed hers. "I had to make myself believe you were that kind of woman, Brook! You had me so confused I couldn't think straight." His eyes, utterly black now with emotion, blazed. "I couldn't let myself believe you were different. I never meant to let any woman get her hooks into me again. I tried every trick I could think of to prove to myself that you were cheap and scheming."

"You were so furious with me," she said softly.

"Because you had gotten to me. Because I was falling in love with you and I thought I could stop myself. I couldn't believe it when you refused me your bed—again and again. God, if you knew how desperately I wanted you!"

She smiled wryly. "You weren't alone, but I'm sure you know that."

Dane scanned her face intently. "I was fool enough to almost let you get away before I admitted to myself that I loved you. Come away from here with me—where we can talk."

Her face became guarded. "It's almost time for me to go to the boarding gate."

"I've said I love you. Doesn't that mean anything to you?"

She reached for her handbag, gripping the handle tightly. "It—it means a great deal. Thank you."

"Thank you!" The words exploded from him angrily.

Quietly she said, "I think perhaps we should find a more private place to finish this conversation." With fingers that shook, she placed money on the table for the coffee, then slid from the booth without looking at him. He followed her from the coffee shop, not speaking, not touching her until she found a quiet lounge area and turned to face him.

"I can't help it," he uttered fiercely. "I can't keep my hands off you any longer." With a moan of pain, he reached out for her, enclosing her in his strong arms. His kiss was fire and desperation. It would always be the same, she thought, as she felt her body quicken with desire under his hungry kiss. Whatever insults he had given her, whatever vile things he had accused her of, he had always had only to touch her to bring her pulses leaping to life and send a consuming fire through her veins.

He ran his fingers through her tumbling hair, cradling her head in his hands as his mouth consumed hers fiercely. "Oh, Brook, I love you," he muttered, lifting his head to devour her with his smoldering eyes. "Say that you love me, too."

Her mouth quivered and she leaned against him for fear of falling. "Do I have to say it? You must know how I feel."

"I want to hear you say the words," he said shortly.

"I love you—I never wanted to and I wish I didn't now."

"Don't, darling—don't have any regrets."

He started to kiss her again, but she turned her face aside. "Please, Dane," she begged, "we have to talk."

His arms encircled her again, and he cradled her head against his shoulder, one hand stroking her hair. "Brook, if you love me, we can work out anything."

"No," she sighed bitterly, "love isn't enough. Love won't solve all problems. You told me once that it only brought pain."

"Didn't you know I was trying to convince myself of that more than you?" His lips brushed her forehead, his breath warm on her skin. "Brook, I want you to be my wife. I need you—Amanda needs you."

Trembling, she pressed her face against his shoulder, her mouth dry. "Dane—oh, Dane, it wouldn't work."

He tilted her chin up, forcing her to look at him. "It will," he said stubbornly.

"You know we'll fight. I could never be like those

184

women I saw on your yacht the day of the picnic. I can't imagine ever giving up my career entirely."

His face relaxed and a smile lit his eyes. "If you ever start acting like one of those women, I'll paddle you! And you can keep your career. We're lucky that you can pursue it anywhere."

She frowned. "But there will be trips—to New York to see publishers, to other places on assignment."

He touched her cheek, his fingers gentle. "I've thought about all that, Brook. I can hire someone to take over some of the work I do now. I've never had a reason to want to hurry home, but when I know you're there, I will. Occasionally, I'll be able to go with you on your assignments. As for the other times, well, I'll just have to get used to having a wife with a career. Just be patient with me, darling, and I'll learn to deal with it."

Dazed, she stared at him. "Oh, Dane—don't be rash. Consider what you're saying. Give yourself some time to think it through."

He shook his head. "I've been doing nothing else for weeks," he muttered. He took her face in his hands. "I won't let you go. Accept that. You're not getting on that plane."

"I have to start another job next week," she said soberly.

He kissed her searchingly. "We'll worry about that next week." He put an arm around her and started walking toward the terminal exit, forcing her to walk along with him. "We should be able to get married in a couple of days. How would you like to be married in Christ Church on St. Simon's? I think it could be arranged. I know somebody on the church board."

Her steps quickened to keep up with his long

strides, and she was smiling. "You know somebody —naturally! You always get what you want, don't you, Dane Darcy?"

"Right," he said in retort, smiling down at her with wicked amusement. "And don't you forget it."

They had reached the terminal exit and passed through. "The car's this way," he told her.

"My clothes," she gasped. "I've already checked my suitcase through."

His stride did not slacken as he looked down at her with a teasing glint in his eyes. "My dear girl, you won't be needing many clothes for a while."

She blushed furiously. "Where are we going now?"

He stopped abruptly on the sidewalk. People were passing them on both sides, but he seemed totally oblivious to anyone but themselves. "We're going back to St. Augustine and get you checked into a hotel. And this time I'm not leaving you at the door." The passionate promise in his eyes made her heart lurch dizzyingly. "Do you hear me, Brook?"

She looked into his eyes, yearning in her face. "I hear you, darling."

And then he kissed her, long and possessively, ignoring the staring passersby with the delighted smiles on their faces.

Silhouette ❦ *Romance*

15-Day Free Trial Offer
6 Silhouette Romances

6 Silhouette Romances, free for 15 days! We'll send you 6 new Silhouette Romances to keep for 15 days, absolutely free! If you decide not to keep them, send them back to us. You pay nothing.

Free Home Delivery. But if you enjoy them as much as we think you will, keep them by paying the invoice enclosed with your free trial shipment. We'll pay all shipping and handling charges. You get the convenience of Home Delivery and we pay the postage and handling charge each month.

Don't miss a copy. The Silhouette Book Club is the way to make sure you'll be able to receive every new romance we publish before they're sold out. There is no minimum number of books to buy and you can cancel at any time.

This offer expires April 30, 1983

Silhouette Book Club, Dept. SBU 17B
120 Brighton Road, Clifton, NJ 07012

Please send me 6 Silhouette Romances to keep for 15 days, absolutely free. I understand I am not obligated to join the Silhouette Book Club unless I decide to keep them.

NAME

ADDRESS

CITY STATE ZIP

Silhouette Romance

Coming next month from
Silhouette Romances

Another Eden by Anne Hampson

Richard was Susanne's world . . . but after the accident had left her blind, it was his brother Nick at her hospital bedside, opening up a brighter future than she ever imagined.

Loving Rescue by Dixie Browning

It was Lacy's first visit to Guatemala . . . her luggage and handbag stolen, was she also in danger of losing her heart to the enigmatic Jordan Stone?

Make-Believe Bride by Nancy John

Would Belinda play substitute wife for Welsh farmer Adam Lloyd when her scheming identical twin walked out on him and Adam mistook her for his new bride?

Runaway Wife by Brenda Trent

When fashion designer Kati Autumn arrived in Mexico City, the last person she expected to meet was Raul, her estranged husband—who wanted her back again.

African Enchantment by Andrea Barry

Armand de Vincent was as exciting and dangerous as Africa itself. How could Patricia be absolutely dedicated to her dancing when she found herself so attracted to this playboy!

Mistletoe And Holly by Janet Dailey

Christmas festivities were the furthest thing from Leslie's mind . . . until she met Tagg and found herself filled with a desire to give the ultimate gift—her heart.

READERS' COMMENTS ON SILHOUETTE ROMANCES:

"I would like to congratulate you on the most wonderful books I've had the pleasure of reading. They are a tremendous joy to those of us who have yet to meet the man of our dreams. From reading your books I quite truly believe that he will someday appear before me like a prince!"

—L.L.*, Hollandale, MS

"Your books are great, wholesome fiction, always with an upbeat, happy ending. Thank you."

—M.D., Massena, NY

"My boyfriend always teases me about Silhouette Books. He asks me, how's my love life and naturally I say terrific, but I tell him that there is always room for a little more romance from Silhouette."

—F.N., Ontario, Canada

"I would like to sincerely express my gratitude to you and your staff for bringing the pleasure of your publications to my attention. Your books are well written, mature and very contemporary."

—D.D., Staten Island, NY

*names available on request